Sholom Aleichem

The Bewitched Tailor

Sholom Aleichem Family Publications

New York

SHOLOM ALEICHEM FAMILY PUBLICATIONS
PO Box 411
Shelter Island, NY 11964
http://www.sholom-aleichem.org

The Bewitched Tailor

ISBN: 1-929068-19-0

CONTENTS

MY FIRST LOVE AFFAIR

Chapter One

I PULL STRINGS AND GET MY FIRST SITUATION

HE WHO HAS had to sit hungry late into the night, muffling himself in a threadbare old coat, poring over a Russian grammar in the light of a bit of candle and declining the noun and adjectives in the phrase "fresh white bread" while he dreams of a crust of ordinary black bread; he who has had to sleep on a hard bench with his head pillowed on his fists, while the lamp smokes, the baby squalls, and the old woman grumbles; he who has had to trudge through thick mud in broken-down boots—one with the heel torn off, the other with a loose floppy sole, which he does not know how to get rid of; he who has tried to pawn his watch which the pawnbroker won't take because it isn't pure silver, and because the works are not worth a pinch of snuff; he who has had to ask a loan from a friend, who, putting his hand in his pocket and drawing out his purse, swears that he hasn't a penny to bless himself with—he who has been through all this, as I have, will no doubt understand how I felt when I got my first situation at twelve rubles a month all found.

I shall not weary you with the story of how I came to get this job, nor need you know that I have an uncle, who has an aunt, who has a friend, who has a kinsman, who has an in-law, who is a very wealthy, though simple man, living in the village. This man has an only son, for whom he wants a private tutor in Yiddish, Russian, German and Book-Keeping. The tutor must be a respectable young man of good family who will not charge too much, not more than they can afford. I make a supreme effort, rush off to my uncle, and ask him to ask his aunt to ask her friend to ask his kinsman to persuade his in-law—the rich man—to hire me and none but me, as there are other young men in Mazepovka besides myself who know Yiddish, Russian, German and Book-Keeping and are prepared to go anywhere to earn a crust of bread. My employer takes quite a time to make up his mind before he consents to have me. For one thing, he is not sure whether he wants a tutor at all, and secondly, he does not know whether to have me or someone else. At last, thank God, he decides in favour of hiring a tutor, and his choice falls upon me, because, if you really want to know, he doesn't attach much importance to learning. Learned men these days, my employer says, are as plentiful as stray dogs. The main thing is that his tutor should be a man from a respectable family, and as I am from a respectable family, he takes me on. That's what my new employer said, but— forgive me for saying so—I'm afraid he lied. My rivals were from families no less "respectable" than mine. Then what is the reason? Just this—influence—the strings.

Yes, the strings are a tremendous power. For blessed is he who hath an uncle, who hath an aunt, who hath a friend, who hath a kinsman, who hath an in-law—a rich man living in the village, who hath an only son for whom he wants a tutor in Yiddish, Russian, German and Book-Keeping, who must be a respectable young man of good family, who will not charge too much, not more than they can afford.

Chapter Two

MY EMPLOYER'S YARNS SEND ME TO SLEEP

Who then was my employer? What did he do for a living? What did he look like? Was he tall or short, fat or thin, ginger or dark? I don't think you need know that. What was his name? That, too, is not so important. He may still be alive, and it would be rather awkward for me to mention names. Let me rather repeat the first conversation I had with him when he invited me into his carriage—a splendid turn-out drawn by a pair of magnificent horses—and treated me to a cigar. It was my first cigar, and that cigar was my undoing.

"So this is your first experience of village life, young man?" he said, studying the grey ash of his black cigar. "I daresay you think that the country is a godforsaken hole and that we village Jews have no taste for good living. Let me tell you, young man, that you will have the pleasure of seeing the real country-house of a rustic Jew—a house with a farmyard, a garden, an orchard —a real palace of a house! As for rooms—front and back, sitting and living—let me tell you, young man, without exaggeration—there are about twenty of them. Twenty, did I say?—why, over thirty! What we want so many rooms for I don't know myself. Unless it's for the guests. I often have guests come to stay with me. Often, did I say? Every week, every day. Not a day passes without some guest arriving, if not two or three. And what guests! The landowner, the *pristav*, the *ispravnik*, the Justice of the Peace.... I'm on friendly terms with the whole neighbourhood. The number of times a four-in-hand comes dashing up to my porch. I ask: Who's that out there? His Excellency, they tell me. That's the *gubernator*, if you know what I mean. Well, naturally, you can't be a pig, you have to receive him decently, give him the best rooms in the house where there's a nice bit of garden. And my garden, let me tell you, is a sight worth seeing! It isn't a garden—it's a forest! You ought to see what apples, what pears, what plums! And the grapes, my dear! I grow all my own things, make wine out of my own cherries and grapes, have my own raisins, and even my own fish out of my own river. And what fish! Carp, tench, bream—breams that size!" My employer spreads his hands wide by way of illustration, and I have to draw back a bit to make room for his breams.

He goes on spinning and spinning his yarns, while I take it all in, hanging on his lips. The carriage rocks like a cradle, the horses jog along at a steady trot, and flick their tails, and I can't say what it is—whether the soft seat in the rocking carriage, the flicking of the horses' tails, or my employer's fibs—only I begin to doze. It is a still summer night. A soft breeze fans my face, and I fall asleep with the sound of my employer's snores in my ears.

By the time we arrived the sun was standing high in the sky. It was a clear sky, clear, bright and cheerful, smiling a welcome to me, the new-comer.

WHAT LIARS THERE ARE. FREEZING LOOKS
AND A WARM RECOMMENDATION

There are different kinds of liars in the world. There are liars who lie readily without having to, for the tongue, as you know, has been made to wag in the mouth. There are three kinds of inveterate liars: the liars of yesterday, the liars of today, and the liars of tomorrow. The liar of yesterday tells you yarns and cock-and-bull stories and swears that he had seen it all with his own eyes—try and prove that he hadn't! The liar of today is not so much a liar really as a braggart. He will assure you that he has everything, knows everything and can do everything—try and verify it if you can. The liar of tomorrow is just a good-natured crank, who will promise you God knows what. He says he will go and see so-and-so for you, do anything for you, and you have to take his word for it. All three kinds of liars know that they are lying, but think that everyone believes them. But there are liars who stand in a class apart. It is enough for one of these to tell a lie for him to believe it himself and to be convinced that others, too, accept it at its face value. Lying gives him great pleasure. These people are fancymongers who live in a land of dreams. They are what you might call story-tellers, making up ever new and new tales, and forgetting today what they had said yesterday. Their fantasy is constantly at work hatching new ideas and thoughts.

To this last category of liars my employer belonged. I need hardly tell you that the palace of his turned out to be just an ordinary house with none too many rooms, and the garden just an ordinary garden as gardens go. Instead of grapes there were green gooseberries, instead of wine—just ordinary cider, instead of whopping breams from the lake—small pikes bought on the market.

We were met by a stout woman carrying a bunch of keys. She looked me over with such a frigid glance that I was taken aback. If looks could speak, hers said: "And who the devil is this?" My employer caught the glance and said in a very meek apologetic tone:

"I have brought a new tutor for the boy. Where is the child?"

"The child is sleeping," she answered in a masculine voice, bestowing another long freezing look upon me. Luckily, the master ordered the table to be laid. He seated me next to him, and during the next few minutes while the samovar was being prepared, told me all about his son—what a good scholar he was, what a beautiful hand he wrote, and what a lot he knew.

"His handwriting is famous here. Everyone enjoys reading his letters. German is his mother tongue! And the way he speaks French!"

The mistress, jingling her keys, served butter, cheese, sour cream, milk, honey and other viands to the table. I would have felt much better, though, if the lady of the house had not sat down opposite me and made me fidget under her kindly glances. My employer intercepted these glances and hastened to explain who and what I was. I felt my face, my eyes, my head and the very hair on my head beginning to tingle. According to him, I was the grandson of the Baal-shem, all my family were rabbis, celebrities and *noggids*, and I myself was better educated than any student, doctor, or professor—better even than three professors rolled into one. I don't know whether she believed these barefaced lies, but her cold hard glance seemed to me to relax a bit.

Chapter Four

THE "CHILD" EATS LIKE A HORSE, WHILE
HIS TUTOR STARVES

My pupil turned out to be a lusty handsome lad of a lively cheerful disposition. He had a round white attractive face with blooming cheeks, a high white forehead, kindly grey eyes, and plump white hands, and there were three things he liked doing: eating, sleeping and laughing. But most of all he liked eating. He ate from morning till night. In between the regular meals of breakfast, lunch, dinner and supper with tea and coffee, his mother kept sending the "child" a *nash* in the shape of a cup of chocolate, or a *beigel*, or a honey-cake, or a pastry, or some preserves, with an occasional titbit such as fried chicken's liver, or other such delicacy, or just a slice of white bread in case he felt peckish, while his tutor looked on and licked his chops and dulled the edge of his appetite with a hand-rolled cigarette.

At first, until he had made friends with his pupil, the tutor experienced the pangs of hunger, for the pupil's mother, the lady with the keys, fed him very sparingly.

They lived in plenty—especially as regards dairy products—but everything was kept under lock and key. Once in a while the master would demand that the tutor should be given something to eat, at which the mistress would start jingling her keys—a sure sign that she was angry.

"But of course!" she would say. "The tutor has his three meals a day. Isn't that enough?"

What a liar she was! I did not have one meal a day, leave alone three. How often did I see chunks of meat thrown away and crocks of milk splashed out, while

I was sitting hungry in my room, dreaming of a piece of black bread. On the days when the master was away I starved. Luckily for me, I quickly made friends with my pupil.

Chapter Five

TUTOR AND PUPIL FORM AN ALLIANCE. THE GAY LIFE STARTS

"Look here, if you want to stay with us, if you want us to become friends," said the "child" to me one fine day, when we were sitting together in his room, the window of which looked out on the garden, "if you don't want to have to leave this place, then chuck those books under the table. We're going to play draughts or 'Sixty-Six,' or let's just loll about in bed and spit at the ceiling."

Saying which, my pupil threw his books under the table, flung himself down on his bed, threw his head back and spat up at the ceiling through his teeth with such skill and marksmanship that we both burst out laughing.

From that day on we had the time of our lives. The pupil taught his tutor to play draughts and "Sixty-Six" (to tell the truth, I had never heard of that card game till then, but when I learned it I became a passionate lover of cards). The tutor formed an alliance with his pupil, and dropping his books and lessons, played draughts or "Sixty-Six" with him, or lay in bed spitting at the ceiling, or helped his pupil to put away the titbits his mother sent him, and managed to do himself quite proud in the process. Happening to glance in the mirror several months later, the tutor was surprised to see how plump he had grown.

No one came into our room except the servant who brought the food. The master of the house was seldom at home, and the mistress, who never let the keys out of her hands, was busy about the house day and night and never looked into our room at all. We really had a good time. We had no cares or obligations, and were free to do what we liked.

But one day my employer asked me, "Well, how are the lessons going?"

"Splendidly," I answered without batting an eyelid.

"There, you see! What did I tell you!" he said, and I was astonished to find that I could still look him in the eye.

In that house, where everyone deceived one another, where everyone lied, where the very air was tainted with lies—in that house it was not difficult for anyone to learn how to lie.

Chapter Six

FIRST LOVE LETTERS OF THE BETROTHED.
THE SPARK IS KINDLED

We nevertheless had one duty to perform—and that was receiving and answering letters. And we received letters almost every day. I say "we" because we both had to answer those letters. The letters to my pupil were written by his betrothed, although he himself admitted to me that his feelings towards her were anything but ardent.

At first the letters did not come very often—once a week, or once a fortnight. But with my arrival upon the scene the correspondence grew more regular and frequent.

"Read that and answer her, will you. What does she want of me?" my pupil said one day, flinging the letter of his beloved into my face. I read it and liked its contents. This is what she wrote:

"My dearest, beloved *fiancé*. If you only knew how weary I am of your letters—they are as like one another as two drops of water from the same river, as if the same mother had given birth to them. I should like to hear some fresh word from you, a word that would warm my heart and illumine my soul.

"My heart is cold, my soul is dark.

"Your devoted *fiancée*...."

Without thinking twice, I penned this answer for my pupil:

"My true bride, beloved. You write that my letters are like each other as if the same mother bore them. How can it be otherwise when one feeling has begotten them? You say that they are as like each other as two drops of water from the same river. How can it be otherwise, when they flow from one source, from one heart? You ask for a fresh word, but what can be fresher than the words "I love"? How can your soul be dark when I think of you, dear love?

"Your devoted *fiancé*...."

To this we soon received the following reply:

"Dear, beloved. Your sweet words have cheered and warmed me, and spread light around me. Assuredly I have heard a new song, the heavenly melody of a dear and loving heart. I feel a different person. It seemed to me as if I had grown wings and was soaring in the heavens, and a host of angels flew out to meet me with great rejoicings and brought me greetings and sweet words from my dear beloved *fiancé*, to whom I belong heart and soul for evermore.

"Your loving and ever faithful bride-to-be...."

"Dearest, sweetest, true love mine," ran my reply.

"No, beloved bride, you were not mistaken. Those were no ordinary cold words, they were feelings that

14

came straight from the heart and found their way to another's heart. They were threads that bound two hearts together with ties eternal. The host of angels that brought you greetings from me, has brought me thine own no less hearty, and with that host I send you back, dear heart, an ardent kiss, the sacred kiss of a friend, who remains your for ever and carries your bright image about in his breast sleeping and waking.

"For ever your devoted lover. . . ."

Chapter Seven

MATERIAL FOR A NEW EPISTOLARY MANUAL

A spark comes flying from God knows where and drops upon a straw-thatched roof. A tiny flame is kindled. The wind fans it into a raging fire. A fire, fire!

Those first letters were the spark from which the hellish flame was kindled. The letters grew ever more ardent. The flame was fanned higher and higher. A great, all-devouring fire raged in my heart; I was ill, terribly ill. I lost my appetite, suffered from insomnia, went about like a lunatic. I poured my heart out in my letters. They were my only solace and joy. The day when I received a letter was a holiday to me. I opened it, read it and wrote a reply. All my pupil had to do was to rewrite it in his own hand, and even so I had to drive him on. And what it cost me to hide the pain away deep down in my heart so as not to betray myself, to bury my face in the pillow and cry softly, then to get up and go about my business with a cheerful mien—to play draughts or a game of "Sixty-Six" with my friend and pupil!

Fortunately, no one noticed that I was suffering, pining away, melting like a candle. Fortunately, my pupil did not take particular note of me. If he had, he would have realized what it was all about, of course. I can imagine the face he would have pulled on seeing me cover his *fiancée*'s letters with kisses. And not to kiss them was impossible!

Judge for yourself. Here is what she writes:

"Angel mine, light of my eyes! I must tell you the whole truth. I must confess, dearest, that I knew you not till now. I never imagined that I would find in you a source of such ardent feelings, such lofty thoughts, such a profound intellect, that I would find in you such a master mind. Your words of wisdom tell me how well-read and educated you are.

"It is surprising that I knew nothing of this before. It speaks of your artless nature and modesty, and raises you still higher in my estimation. How can I help feeling happy when fate has bound up my lot with a man in whom all the finest qualities are exemplified: beauty, intellect, knowledge, simplicity of heart and goodness. Your goodness shows itself in your sweet wise words. You bestow your dear letters upon me with a generous hand. I thank you for them a thousand times, and beg for more.

"Your true-love, eternally yours...."

To this I replied somewhat hazily:

"My dearest, beloved, beautiful, clever one! You knew me not because you had not seen me. The one you have seen is not I, but my reflection. Imagine that we have only just made each other's acquaintance, that we have not yet seen one another, that we have been born anew, as it were. How happy are we not to know this world, this false despicable world and the false despicable creatures who people it.

"Your loving *fiancé*, faithful unto death...."

I received from her the following reply:

"My beloved, dearest, heaven-sent angel mine! Your letter was a seven-sealed book to me, a riddle. You write so obscurely that I had to cudgel my brains for a long time to grasp your meaning, and now I believe I can proudly say that I understand you fully. You say that we should consider ourselves happy for not knowing this false despicable world with its false despicable people. I must be one of the unhappy ones then, because I do know this false despicable world with its false despicable people. And what bliss it is to realize that there exists at least one honest, noble-hearted man, truthful, wise and tender, and that that man is my betrothed, my heaven-sent lover! Be well, my dearest, write me what you are reading now and what books you would recommend me to read.

"I press your hand with affection and remain forever your true-love...."

My reply was as follows:

"My life, my heart, my paradise! If I have surprised you so, then imagine what a riddle and what a revelation you must have been to me. I never dreamt that I would receive such letters from you. Judging from the occasional Hebrew words which you use in your letters, I see that our ancient language is not unknown to you. For that alone I think so highly of you that I almost fear to be unworthy of uttering your very name! I gaze upon your photograph and say to myself: there she is, a real Jewish girl. There is my ideal, and I am prepared to sacrifice my life for you every minute of the day. You ask what to read? I am sending you a list of well-known Russian and foreign classics, such as Gogol, Turgenev, Tolstoi, Dostoyevsky, Pushkin, Lermontov, Shakespeare, Goethe, Schiller, Heine, Burns. I hope they give you pleasure. Answer me quickly. The day when I receive a letter from you is a holiday to me. Be well, dearest, be well, my true-love.

"Your affectionate and devoted lover...."

And this is what she answered:

"Crown of my head, treasure mine, light of my life!

"I don't understand why the few Hebrew words in my letters should have surprised you so. Ancient Hebrew is our national capital, our treasury. Is the knowledge of that language to be held a special merit in a Jewish girl? It would be a shame and disgrace if she could not recite by heart a few verses of Jehuda Halevi, if, upon finishing college, she did not know Mapu, Levinsohn, Smolenskin, Gordon and other Hebrew classics! I thank you very much for the list you sent me, although I read all these classics a long time ago. Besides these I have also read such famous writers and poets as Byron, Swift, Cervantes, Dickens, Thackeray, Shelley, Balzac, Daudet, Hugo, Sienkiewicz, Orzeszkowa, etc., etc. I wanted something new and fresh, not a novel, but something serious. Be well, my beloved, my sweet. Do not set me on too high a pedestal. I am just an ordinary girl, devoted to you body and soul.

"Your true-love...."

To which I replied....

But have we not had enough of this lovers' correspondence? I am afraid otherwise this will turn out to be an epistolary manual instead of a novel. I should like to add, however, that I still preserve all these letters in a secret corner of my desk. No human eye except my own has seen them. They are as dear to me as the age-old leaves of some remote chronicle, silent witnesses to my first joys and my first anguish. They are the dried and withered flowers on the grave of my first love, my first romance.

Chapter Eight
I BECOME A HARDENED LIAR

When a man is in love you can always tell it by his face. Just look how his eyes wander, how strangely he smiles, how absent-mindedly he answers, how he looks at himself in the mirror every minute of the day, how he puts on a different neckerchief every day, how light and springy his step is, how he loves the whole world—if he were not so shy he would have kissed the chimney-sweep.

But no one was watching me. True, my pupil sometimes asked me during a game of draughts why I was so absent-minded and took my own men instead of his. I would answer in surprise, "What men?" My employer, too, once asked me at the table why I looked so bad. At which the mistress, jingling her keys, answered (with a look of pity on her face, although inwardly she was glad) that the tutor hardly ate anything lately.

"What's the matter?" the master asked, and answered for me himself: "You work too hard, that's what. You two are sitting indoors all day long, poring over your books. You ought to go out for walks."

"How can we go for walks when we have so much to do?" my pupil said with such genuine innocence that I wanted to spit in his face and shout out at the top of my voice, "People! How can you be such liars! The air in this house is thick with your lies!"

But I did not say it. Instead of telling the truth I told another lie.

"I miss my people."

"That's not surprising," said my employer, rallying to the support of my fibs with the full force of his rich imagination. "He has someone to miss, I tell you. His family is the leading family in their town and outside of it. I don't mind telling you that you won't find another family like it in all the district. The Kovno rabbi is a relation of yours, I believe, isn't he?"

"My uncle," I lied shamelessly.

"And the *maggid* from Porechie is also an uncle of yours, I think?"

"Yes, on mother's side," I answered.

"And Epstein, the great Epstein, is related to you, too, isn't he?"

"Yes, we are cousins," I said.

"And Moishele Galperin is also a kinsman of yours, I believe?"

"Yes, on my father's side," I answered.

"*Nu*, and the Tolchin *noggids*, I heard, are also near relations of yours?"

"Second cousins," I said.

And I am terribly glad, not so much at having acquired such a grand *mishpocha*, as at my being left alone at last to the solitude of my rapturous and sacred feelings, and the sweet delightful letters of my pupil's *fiancée*, who is dearer to me than all my real and imaginary relatives, near and distant.

This is what she wrote me in one of her further letters:

"My delight, my heavenly angel!

"Wherefore this gloom? Why are your last letters so sad? Why do you speak of death? What mean these riddles that you pose me? Why do you consider yourself to be the unhappiest of unhappy mortals? Why do you cause me so much suffering? Why do you not reveal to me the great secret that is eating your heart out? What secrets can you have from her who loves you alone and no one else, who eagerly counts the days until we meet and are happily united for ever and ever!!!"

From the *fiancé* came the following reply:

"My sacred soul, the apple of my eye! My idol!

"I beg you, forgive me for those last letters of mine. Forget that I ever wrote them. You are right, my dearest, you are right! I have no right to complain, no right to call myself unhappy. He is unhappy who has never loved and been loved. I repeat again that your letters are my only joy, that it were bliss to me to see you and

20

die. But no, I have sworn to speak of death no more. You want to know my great secret? O no, you will not know it until that happy (or unhappy) hour strikes when we shall see each other before the marriage ceremony. Then you will know all.... Meantime, be well, my dearest, my sacred heart, and write, write, write!

"Your happy and unhappy lover, who, O, so wants this time to drag on...."

Chapter Nine

PREPARATIONS FOR THE WEDDING AND MY SILLY DREAMS

He who has ever loved will understand what I felt when the time came for making preparations for the wedding. And he who has carefully read the foregoing chapters will understand how I felt when my pupil had his wedding suit fitted in the course of three weeks running. The tortures of the damned are nothing to what I suffered. Gehenna would have seemed an Eden compared to my anguish.

You probably think that all these feelings were born of hatred towards a lucky rival. Nothing of the kind! I knew only too well that it was not my pupil who was loved, but myself, the real author of those letters. I knew only too well that I had but to reveal the secret, the sacred secret, at our first meeting, to breathe but a word, and she would understand at once, and everything would turn out for the best. But how was it to be done? How could I arrange to speak to her in private, if only for a few minutes? I racked my brains, devised probably seventeen thousand ridiculous plans, one more fantastic and crazy than the other. Frankly, such wicked thoughts came into my head that I feel ashamed to set them down in writing even though no little time has elapsed since then. You think I intended murdering my rival, poisoning him? God spare such sinful thoughts! I only prayed God for some miracle to happen—for my pupil to fall ill and be gathered to his fathers so that I could step into his place.

To tell you the truth, I brooded over it day and night, hoping and longing that my pupil would catch his death of cold sitting in a draught, or that some cough or ague would seize him, or that he would slip on an even spot and break his neck, or that his head by chance would stop some flying stone, or that a mad dog would bite him and he'd go dotty, or that a storm would tear up a tree and drop it straight on his head, or that some other miracle would happen, I don't care what, so long as I was rid of him.

At the same time I felt a twinge of remorse and was sorry for him. Why should he suffer, an innocent soul? Why should he die so young? At heart I wept over him, sincerely bemoaned him. I wrote my beloved darling a letter ending in a sorrowful verse, in which I seriously lamented the tragic death of my poor young pupil. I compared the world to a cemetery, and him to a young tree:

The nightingale stands there weeping away,
And the stars are pouring tears....

There was some more, but I don't remember it.

And once again my imagination paints me other scenes: a year has passed since his death, and I and my beloved have come to his grave to shed a tear and place fresh sweet-smelling flowers upon it; we have even dedicated some verses to him, which end thus:

Let the flowers bloom upon thy grave,
And let thy soul repose in paradise....

Whether the flowers will bloom on his grave is extremely doubtful, but that my pupil is blooming like a rose—is a fact. His health improves from day to day, his face grows ruddier and his body plumper. He was pleased, elated, cheerful and happy—happy not from love, but from the fact that he was moving out to a big town where he would meet new people and see no more of his tiresome kinsfolk.

He admitted as much to me on more than one occasion, although, to their face, he told his parents that he would miss them terribly.

"Will you miss me, too?" I asked him.

"Of course!" he answered, embracing me in a friendly way. "But I will take you with me. We'll have a good time together. We'll play draughts and go to the theatre. I'll never part with you, never!"

I knew it was a barefaced lie. Born, reared and educated on lies, he had lied again.

Chapter Ten

I AM INVITED TO THE WEDDING

I shall never forget the attention paid us when we arrived for the wedding. A splendid carriage, waiting for us at the station, took us to a handsome house, where we were given separate rooms, treated to delicious coffee and cakes and an excellent luncheon of fried eggs and roast duck. And the crowd, the crowd! And ever more people kept coming to greet us and make our acquaintance.

To my dazed mind they were like a swarm of tiny insects, scurrying about and buzzing like flies. I was engrossed in my thoughts, the most cheerless of thoughts—how to see her in private. Who knows whether I would succeed! What if she discovered my sacred secret? And what if—I dare not even pronounce it..., It is terrible, terrible!

I had slipped into my pocket beforehand on leaving the house—don't be scared, not a revolver, heaven forbid, but a letter "to her," a letter on three pages describing the story of my love together with a short autobiography. But how was I to deliver that letter to her? Through whom? And when would she be able to read it?

Meanwhile all her kinsfolk, men and women, bustled and rushed about like poisoned rats, driving the servants, hurrying the preparations for the wedding feast, sending for the musicians and the rabbi. Hurry up with the ceremony—the bride and bridegroom must be faint with fasting, poor things!

That the bridegroom did not fast—I know for a fact. He had polished off a goodly portion of roast duck in my room, and afterwards pretended that he was fasting, pulling a lenten face as becomes a bridegroom and trying to look as if he were wrapped in some serious thought or other.

Born, reared and educated on lies, he lied even on his wedding-day.

Meanwhile the musicians had arrived and the ceremony of veiling the bride was begun. The noise and bustle were terrific! Everyone made believe that he was busy doing something. "Quick! Quick! Come on! Hurry up!" And someone—we know not who—led us away—we know not where, and someone spoke to us—we know not what; I felt dizzy and dazed, my ears rang, and my heart thumped—tick-tock, tick-tock....

The musicians played, the fiddle sobbed, the trumpet blared, the flute whistled, the drums boomed bum-bum, bum-bum, and my heart went tick-tock, tick-tock.

Chapter The Last

THE "EPILOGUE" OF A ROMANCE

Among the faces that floated dizzily before my eyes I noticed one that looked as much a stranger to the place as I did. It belonged to a long-haired young man in spectacles, whose sole occupation was to watch and observe all that was going on. He looked as if he was enjoying it too!

His glance came to rest upon me, and I felt that he saw right through me, saw my heart, my secret, my sacred secret—and I dropped my eyes. Nevertheless I was keenly aware of his intent gaze fixed upon me; I felt him staring at me steadily all the time, and looking up, I caught a glance that pierced my heart and drew me like a magnet.

I don't know how it happened, but we found ourselves standing together—I and the young man in the spectacles, and we dropped into conversation, naturally, about the wedding—about the bride and the bridegroom.

The parents took the bridegroom under the elbows and led him up to the bride. She was sitting on a chair in the middle of the room with her hair down and her face buried in her hands—as if weeping. The musicians played away, the fiddle sobbed, the trumpet blared, the flute whistled, the drum boomed—bum-bum-bum, and my heart went tick-tock, tick-tock.

"Another minute, another minute," I thought, "and it will all be over."

"A cow!" the young man in the spectacles suddenly whispered into my ear.

"Where?" I said, looking round.

"There she is," he answered, jerking his glasses towards the bride.

Seeing the look of utter bewilderment on my face, he whispered:

"A cow, a real cow. She doesn't know a thing, and she's spiteful as can be. Marrying a good fellow like that too. You are his tutor, I believe."

I don't know whether it was I who took him aside, or he me, or both of us together, but within a couple of minutes we were sitting side by side like old acquaintances. The young man in the spectacles—the bride's tutor—was telling me things about her that I had been much happier for not knowing.

"But look at her letters!" I cried. "What about her letters?"

At these words the young man in the spectacles held his sides with laughter.

"Her letters? Ha, ha, ha! Her letters! Oh, what a scream! Are those her letters?"

"Then whose are they?"

"Hers? Ha, ha, ha! Her letters! Mine! Ha, ha, ha! They're mine! Mine! Mine!"

I thought the young man had gone mad or something. He seized my hands, spun round the room, slapped me on the back, and laughed without a stop.

"Her letters, ha, ha, ha! Her letters!"

Have you ever had a bright dream about a beautiful castle with good angels, excellent wines, fruit fresh off the trees, sweet scents, paradise—and "she," the princess with the golden locks. And you soar skyward, up and up into the heavens. Then suddenly the vision fades. From the forest comes a harsh whistle, a flapping of wings, a wild weird burst of laughter—ha, ha, ha; it echoes through the forest and breaks off at the fringe like a suppressed yawn: A-a-a! At your feet yawns an abyss. In another moment you will go hurtling down. With a start, you wake up, wake up with a splitting headache, and it is quite a time before you come to your-self.

Such was the dream I had in that brief flash during which the young man stood before me laughing, laughing without a stop at my letters and going over all the excellent qualities of my beloved. He laughed, whilst my heart bled.

In the hall the musicians were playing. The fiddle sobbed, the trumpet blared, the flute whistled, the double-bass droned, the drum boomed: bum-bum-bum! And in my heart was dark desolation, emptiness.

1903

T H E   T H R E E   W I D O W S

THE STORY OF A GRUMPY OLD BACHELOR

1

WIDOW NUMBER ONE

OU ARE wrong, my dear sir—not all old maids are unhappy, not all old bachelors are egoists. You sit in your study with a cigar in your mouth and a book in your hands, and you think you have plumbed all the hidden depths of the human soul, you know all there is to know, and there are no more unsolved problems for you. Especially when, with God's help, you have hit on such a saving word as Psychology. What a word —Psy-chol-o-gy! But do you know what Psychology is? There is a vegetable called parsley.... To look at it's not bad, it smells nice, tastes good when you flavour food with it. Now Psychology is much the same as parsley. But you try chewing parsley by itself! You don't want to? Then why do you stick Psychology down my throat? If you want to know what Psychology really is, then kindly sit down and listen carefully to what I am going to tell you. After that you can offer your opinion as to whence all the world's ills and evils come from wherein lie the causes of egoism, and so forth.

Take me, for instance. An old bachelor I am, and an old bachelor I shall die. Why? Because there are special reasons for it. Once you ask me why, and are ready to hear me out—there's the real Psychology for you. Only one thing I ask—do not interrupt me with questions: who? what? when? I hate to be interrupted. I'm not without my whims, as you know, and lately my nerves are not quite in order. Don't be frightened—I haven't gone mad. You are more likely to do that than I am—you are a married man. Besides, I can't afford it, I have to keep sane and healthy. I must. You'll say so yourself. In a word then, no questions please. When I have told you the whole story, and there is anything that still does not seem clear to you, then you can lodge your complaint, by all means. *Nu?* Is that all? Well, then, sit down here in my place, and I'll sit in your rocking-chair, if you don't mind. I like it soft and comfortable, too, you know. And it will be better for you as well—you won't fall asleep.

And so, to begin my story. I hate preliminaries and idle chatter.

Her name was Paya, and she was called "the young widow." Why? There we go now—why, wherefore? It's clear enough, surely! Once she was called the "'young widow," it means that she was young and that she was a widow. I was younger than her. By how much? What's the difference? I say I was younger, so I was younger. To cut a long story short, there were people with wagging tongues who started gossiping about me being a bachelor and her being a young widow. You follow me? Some people even congratulated me and wished me joy. You can believe me or not—I don't care whether you do or don't. I see no reason for boasting before you. I was as intimate with her as you are with me.... We were just good friends and were fond of each other. Nothing surprising in that. I had known her husband. And not only known him, but had been friendly with him. I don't say that we had been friends. I said we had been friendly. These are two different things: you can be friendly, but not be friends, and, the other way about, you can be very close friends and not be friendly. That's my opinion. You can keep yours to yourself. Well then, her husband and I were friendly, we played cards together, sometimes chess. They say I am a first-rate chess-player. I don't want to boast. There may be better chess-players than me. I'm only telling you what people say. Her husband was a young man, a smart, clever, and what's more a well-informed one, an extremely well-informed man, I should say. Self-taught. Didn't study in any of those colleges or universities of yours, didn't take any degrees. All those degrees of yours are not worth a *grosh*! What? You don't agree? Then don't! You won't catch me arguing. He was rich, very rich. Although I don't know what your idea of being rich is. With us a Jew who has a house of his own, a turn-out, and a business on top of it, is considered a wealthy man. We make no fuss and noise, and don't show off, we go our way quietly, slowly, you know. Well then, he had a business and made a nice living. Calling on them was a great pleasure—you were always sure of a welcome. Not like some people, who, the first time you call, don't know where to seat you; the next time you call they don't make half such a fuss, and the third time they receive you so coldly that you're liable to catch a chill. You needn't smile, I'm not hinting at anybody we know When you go there, they give you to eat and drink, and treat you like one of the family. What more do you want? For instance, if, excuse me, a button comes off, they will sew it on for you right away. You laugh? You think it funny. A button? What is a button? A button, let me

tell you, is a big thing for us bachelors! A whole world!
A nasty thing happened once through a button: a young
man came to the bride-show, and someone pointed to
a missing button of his and passed a sneering remark
about it. That young man went home and hanged himself. But let us get on with the story—I hate to drag
in all kinds of subjects. And they lived, did the husband and wife, like a pair of doves. They made a better
go of it, let me tell you, than many of those modern
young couples of yours, even those amongst the highest
ranks. I'm not criticizing anybody. If you have a different opinion you're welcome to it. Well then, to get on
with the story.

One day Pinye, that's Paya's husband, comes home,
takes to his bed, stays there five days, and on the sixth
—no more Pinye! Who? What? When? Don't ask. A boil
came out on his neck, it had to be cut open, but it wasn't.
Why? Because! That's what doctors are for. I brought
two doctors to him, and they started arguing. One in-
sisted on having it cut open, the other says—no. While
they were having it out the patient goes and dies. So
there you are. Sometimes, when you think of the number of people they have sent to the next world your
hair stands up on end. They poisoned my own sister.
You think they gave her poison? I'm not a madman to
say such foolish things. When I say poisoned her, I
mean they didn't give what they should have given
her. If they had given her quinine in time she might
have still been alive. Don't worry, I know where I left
off. Well then, we lost our friend Pinye. Who can express the sorrow? I would not have been half so sorry if
it had been my own brother, my father! To think of it—
Pinye! It was as if years, many years of my life had
been taken away from me. And the pain of it! The misfortune! And the widow! Left with a tiny infant on her
hands—little Rosa, an angel. Our only comfort! If not

for the child I don't know how we could have borne it—she and I. I'm not a woman, not a mother, to make a fuss of her child without rhyme or reason. But if I tell you that that child was one in a million—then you can take my word for it she was. You couldn't look at her long enough. In a word, she was the love fruit of two remarkably beautiful people. I don't know who was the better—he or she. Pinye was handsome, Paya was lovely. The child had her father's eyes—blue ones. We both loved the child, but I don't know who loved her best—she or I. I ask you—is such a thing possible? She the mother, I a stranger? That doesn't prove anything. You've got to look deeper: my attachment to the house, my pity for the widow, sympathy for the poor, sweet, fatherless child, and the fact that I was all alone in the world—all this, taken together, is the thing that you call Psychology. Not parsley, but Psychology pure and simple. Perhaps you will say it was because I loved the mother? I did, I don't deny it. Do you know how I loved her? I pined for love of her, but I dared not hint as much. I lay awake night after night, thinking how to tell her. I would get up in the morning resolved, it seemed, to go and tell her straight: "I would like you to know, Paya,—so-and-so and so-and-so. As for the rest, decide yourself. . . ." But when you go there the words don't come. You will say I am a coward? Say what you like. But try to look below the surface: Pinye was my friend, I loved him better than a brother. "And Paya?" you will ask. "Didn't you say just now that you were pining for her?" Exactly, I will answer you. Just because I pined for her, because I loved her to distraction, I could not pluck up the courage to tell her so. I'm afraid you won't understand me, though. Of course, if I were to fall back on that Psychology of yours you would understand me quick enough, but when you tell the simple straightforward story from a pure heart it sounds crazy.

Think what you like—what do I care! To continue then. The child grew up. To say that it "grew," of course, is to say nothing. A child grows, a tree grows, and so does a turnip. There's a difference, though. You live only for the day when that child will sit up, and stand, and walk, and run, and speak! Then, at last, it does sit up, it does stand, and walk, and run, and speak. So what? You don't expect me to turn an old wife and start talking chicken-pox to you, and measles, and teething and all the rest of it? I'm not a woman to prattle foolishness, and tell you about childish pranks either. The little girl grew up and blossomed "like a tender rose," I would say, if I wanted to use the language of you novelists, who know as much about blooming roses as a cow of Sunday. They are better at sitting in their studies, you know, warming their feet at the stove and describing nature, the green woods, the stormy seas, the sandy mountains, last-year's snow. Such writings are disgusting. They make me sick. I don't read them. When I pick up a book and find the sun shining in it, the moon riding the skies, the air fragrant, and the birds twittering—I throw that book on the floor. You laugh? You think I'm a psychopath? Think what you like!

So she grew up, did Rosa, and received a proper education, as befits an intellectual home. Her mother saw to that, and I, too, gave a little attention to her education. A little, did I say? I don't mind telling you I gave quite a lot of my attention to the child, practically all my time, in fact. I saw to it that she had the best teachers, that she was never late for school, that she played the piano, that she learned to dance—I attended to all that, I did, all alone. Who else was there? I also handled the widow's affairs, otherwise she would have gone to ruin, she would! Those Jews of yours fleeced her enough as it was. I know you will feel sore about me saying "those Jews." But what *can* I say when there are such people? You can call me an anti-Semite as much as you like, but I have my own mind about it. May the anti-Semites have as many plagues as I know what a Jew is. If you want to know a Jew, ask me. I haven't had much to do with them myself. As you know, I have my own houses and my own shops, from which I make a nice income, and that's enough for me. Even so, I have to sing a song every time a lease has to be renewed, a house repaired, or rent collected. The gentiles, let me tell you, are no better. But you'd expect a Jew to be above that. After all, the Chosen People, you know. You think that by singing their praises as the Chosen People you are doing them a service? Nothing of the sort! What? You can't stand it? I don't want to start an argument with you. You say it's not so—all right, let it be not so. Everyone is entitled to his own opinion. Other people's opinions don't bother me at all. I know my own mind.

After Pinye's death a whole horde of mean people—well-wishers, advisors and what not—came down on her and began to fleece the poor woman the way they usually do. It's good that I put my foot down in time—Stop!—and took all her affairs in hand. True, she wanted me to go into partnership with her, but I flatly refused. I wasn't going to sell my houses and have headaches. There's no need to sell your houses, she says, you could become my partner just like that. And what do you think I said to that? I told her never to make me any such offers again, otherwise I'd get angry. "He," I says —may his soul rest in peace—"he doesn't deserve that I should make you pay me for my trouble, and as for the time I am giving to your affairs," says I, "I take no money for that. I have plenty of time," I says, "more than I know what to do with." I tell her that, and she, the widow, doesn't say a word. Just drops her eyes and says nothing. If you understand anything at all, you ought to guess what I meant. Why didn't I say it straight out? Don't ask me. The fact remains that I didn't. One thing I can tell you—it was as simple as lighting this cigarette here. One word—and we would have been married. But I thought: What about Pinye? We were such friends! I know what you want to say—the love between us could not have been so very great. You are wrong. That I was pining for her, I already told you, but that she for me, I had rather say nothing, in case you thought—Oh, but what do I care what you think! Tell them to bring some tea, my throat is getting dry.

Now where were we, my dear sir, if you remember? Affairs, yes. Affairs, I tell you! I'll remember them as long as I live. Talk about exploitation, and twisting people round one's little finger! Wait a minute, don't be so glad! Not me—her! You can't twist me round your little finger so easily. And shall I tell you why? Because I won't stand for it. But stand for it or not, what can you do when you have to deal with swindlers, crooks and bandits, who can cheat the devil himself? They tried their damnedest to grab all they could. But as you can well imagine, it's no easy job to get money out of me. They had the devil of a time, I can tell you, and were spitting blood before they could pump or screw out of me—do you know how much? As much as they could! It was good I put my foot down in time, and said to the widow: Enough, I says, that'll do! And I put a clean stop to it, just cut it off with a knife! Even so, she lost a good bit. You will ask—why did I allow it? I'd like to see how you would have got out of it in my place. Maybe you would have done better, I am not saying. Maybe people will say of me—he's not much of a businessman. I should worry! Better a bad businessman than a bandit. You think it didn't cost me a pretty penny too? But I don't want to boast about it. All I want to tell you is how things worked out so's the widow should not remain a widow and I an old bachelor. I only had to tell her one word ... but that one word was never uttered. Why? That's just it. That's where the real Psychology stuff comes in. A new chapter under the heading "Rosa"! You just listen carefully, don't miss a word, because this isn't a piece of fiction, you understand, it's a slice of life—real, warm, throbbing life.

I don't know why it is, but every mother's mind has a peculiar twist. As soon as a girl grows out of her short frocks, her mother is all agog to see her engaged as soon as possible. And when the mother sees young men dangling after her daughter, she is just crazy with excitement and joy. Every young man is a possible *fiancé* to her. That that *fiancé* may be a good-for-nothing, a charlatan, a gambler, a God knows what—doesn't worry her in the least. You may be sure, we had no charlatans and chatterboxes coming to our place, first of all because Rosa was not the kind of girl who has anything to do with those dancing dudes who wriggle about, cut capers on the parquet, crook their elbows, scrape a leg and bend the neck. Secondly, what am I there for? Can you see me allowing any popinjay to get within three feet of Rosa? Why, I'd have broken all the man's bones for him, I would! I went to a ball with her once at the Jewish club among the real aristocracy, you know, those you call the bourgeoisie. Well, up comes one of those fops—elbow crooked, head cocked, on his face a honeyed little smile, scrapes a leg, speaks in a high girlish voice. The devil knows what he said. Asking for a dance, it seems. Well, I showed him a dance, I tell you! He'll remember me! Did we laugh afterwards at that poor spark! Since then, all the beaux knew that before making Rosa's acquaintance, they had me to deal with first, to pass, so to speak, an examination, and not till then could they go while the going was good. They called me Cerberus, that is, the watchdog at the gates of paradise. I should worry! But do you know who was angry on this account? Her mother. "You are scaring people away," she says, "you don't let anyone come near." "What people?" says I. "Those are not people, they're dogs." That happened a few times. Once it nearly ended in a catastrophe. You think we quarrelled? You're a clever man, I admit, but this time you have guessed wrong. You just listen what happened.

One day I come to the widow's house and find a guest there—a young man of about twenty or thirty. There are such young men, you know—you can never tell how old they are. He was a very nice chap, though, I must say. There are such likeable chaps—nice face, nice eyes —nothing to pick on. I took a fancy to him right away. Do you know why? Because I can't stand fellows with sugary faces and honeyed little smiles. I hate those nasty fawning yes-men, who peer into your eyes and agree with everything you say. Tell them that it snowed in July or that a fish grew on a tree, and they'll even agree with you in that. When I see a creature like that I feel like smearing honey over him and letting the bees have a go at him. You want to know what the name of that young man was? What difference does it make? Well, let's say it was Shapiro. Does that satisfy you? And he was the bookkeeper at the distillery, and not just the bookkeeper, but the absolute boss; as a matter of fact he had a bigger say at the works than the employer himself. An employer who doesn't trust his employees doesn't deserve to be an employer. You may have other ideas on that score—that's your business.

To cut a long story short, they introduced to me a young man by the name of Shapiro, a bookkeeper, a manager, a respectable man, and an excellent chess-player at that. He played chess no worse, if not better, than I did. As I told you, I don't consider myself a great chess-player. Well, who was to know that a love affair was in the making here, and what a love affair! A grand passion! And ass that I was, I didn't notice anything! Can you imagine it—I poured oil on the flames with my own hands, I lauded this man to the skies! May it burn in a fire, that chess, with all the world's chess-players to boot! While we were playing chess, he had something else at the back of his mind all the time. I took his Queen while he took my Rosa. I checkmated him in ten moves, but he mated me in three, because at the fourth move, that is, when he came the fourth time, the widow called me aside, and, with a peculiar light in her eye, informed me that Rosa had become engaged to this same Shapiro and that she was in her seventh heaven. In a word—congratulate me, and yourself, and the two of us.

What happened to me when this glad news was broken to me, I had better not say. You'll say I am a villain, a madman, a crazy fellow? That's what she said, too—the widow, that is. At first she laughed, then she started shouting at me, and the end of it was tears, hysterics and all the rest—in a word, a conflict! The blister burst, you understand. We had it out between us and said more cruel truths to each other in half an hour than we had ever uttered in all the twenty years we had known each other. I told her flatly that she was my evil genius, that she had ruined my life, taken away my only comfort in life—Rosa, and given her to another. At which she said that if ever anyone had tried to steal the soul of another, then it was I who had been doing that little by little in the course of eighteen odd years! What she meant, I need not explain to you—even a fool would understand it. But what I answered her, I will not tell you. All I will say is that I did not treat her in a gentlemanly way, which is as good as saying that I was rude to her, very rude. I snatched my hat, ran out like a madman and slammed the door.

And I swore never again to cross that threshold as long as I lived. Well, what do you say? You are a thinking man, aren't you? What does your Psychology have to say about that? What should I have done—drowned myself? Or bought myself a revolver? Or hanged myself on the nearest tree? That I didn't drown, shoot, or hang myself, you can see yourself, thank God. What happened next? I'll tell you about that next time. Nothing will happen to you if you wait a bit. I have to go to see my widows. They're expecting me for dinner.

So much for widow number one.

2

WIDOW NUMBER TWO

Why did I keep you waiting so long? Well, I just wanted to, that's all. If you are going to tell anything then tell it in your own time. That you've got nothing against listening, anyone can see. Everyone likes a story, especially when it's an interesting one. What's wrong, say, with my sitting in my room after dinner in an armchair, a cigar in my mouth, while you talk yourself into a fever to amuse me? And what do you care if the story-teller, maybe, is suffering in the telling of it? All you care about is to hear an interesting story. I don't mean you, keep your hair on. Just listen then attentively. And although what I'm going to tell you now has nothing to do with the previous story, still, I'd like you to remember what I told you last time, because there *is* some connection between them, and very much so, if it comes to that. And if you have forgotten anything I'll remind you. Here then is the previous story in a few words.

I had a friend named Pinye. Pinye had a wife named Paya and a daughter named Rosa. My friend died, leaving Paya a young widow to whom I was a near friend, a secretary, a brother. I pined for love of her. But I did not have the pluck to tell her. So passed the best years of our life. The daughter grew up, Rosa bloomed, and I lost my peace of mind, was smitten. The devil brought a young man, a bookkeeper by the name of Shapiro, who played a fair game of chess, and Rosa fell in love with him. All the resentment that rankled in my breast I vented on her mother. I slammed the door and swore never to cross that threshold again as long as I lived. Well, are you satisfied?

There's one thing you are dying to know, I am sure, and that is, did I keep my word or not? But, of course, you're a "psychologist." Tell me—should I have kept my word or not? You are silent? Shall I tell you why? Because you don't know yourself. This is what happened then.

I walked about the town all night like a lunatic, measuring the streets up and down, then went home at daybreak, looked over all my papers, tore up many of them—I can't stand old papers lying about—packed my things and wrote a few letters to some acquaintances— I have no friends or relations, thank God, I'm all alone in the world. I left orders about the disposal of my houses and shops, and that done, I sat down on the bed with bent head and thought, thought and thought until morning came. Then I had a wash, everything right and proper, dressed, and went off to see my widow. I rang the bell, walked in, ordered coffee, and began waiting for the widow to get up. The widow soon got up. At the sight of me she stopped for a minute. Her eyes were swollen, her face was pale. Had she, too, spent a sleepless night?

"How is Rosa?" I asked.

Just then Rosa came into the room. Fresh and lovely as God's day, sweet and smiling as the bright sun. At sight of me she blushed slightly, then went up to me, stroked my head with her little hand, the way you would a child, then peered into my eyes and laughed. And how, think you, did she laugh? Not, God forbid, offensively, but in such a way that you wanted to laugh yourself, and everything around, even the walls, seemed to smile back. Yes, my dear sir, that's the power that Rosa possesses even to this day. Even now I'd willingly give up everything I have to hear her laugh. The trouble is she laughs no more. She is past laughter. But I must not run forward. Once I start a thing I like to go on with it in proper order.

Well then, let's take it in order.

Do you know what it is to marry a daughter? No? You don't? May God help you from ever knowing it. I've had the experience, I know what it is, even though she wasn't my own daughter. I won't forget it very quickly. But what, I ask you, could I do, when my widow, that is, Paya, was used to having everything brought home to her on a platter? And whose fault was it if not my own? Whenever anything was wanted in the house, no matter what, they always used to come to me—the mother and the daughter. The world could turn upside down —everything they wanted had to be delivered, and not later than in two hours! Money is wanted—they come to me. A doctor—me. A cook—me. A dancing master— me. Dresses, shoes, the tailor, the butcher, a nib, a hook —it was always me, me, me! You think I didn't reproach them with it, "What will be with you? You'll become a rag!" I talk to them, and they laugh—hee, hee, hee, ha, ha, ha— they think it very funny. And so all their lives. There are such people in the world, you know. Not many, but there are. And who, of all men, was to have them on his head? I! Who was to have the care of other men's children? I was. Who was to suffer through other people's troubles? I was. Who was to dance at someone else's weddings? I was. Who was to weep at other people's funerals? I was. You will ask me—what made me do it? To which I will answer you: what makes you dash into a burning house to save someone else's child? What makes you wince when someone else is in pain? You will tell me that you don't do either the one or the other? In that case you are a brute. And I am not a brute, I'm a human being. I do not pretend to be an idealist, I'm just an ordinary man, and an old bachelor at that. Now your Psychology claims that old bachelors are egoists. Maybe, though, it *is* egoism in a way? What? You don't like to probe, to philosophize? No more do I.

Well then Rosa, the daughter of my widow, had to be married and I had to act the blessed *shadchan*. What else was there for me to do? From what you already know of me you can well imagine how I liked doing it! The very word *shadchan* makes me feel sick. Call me a "man," call me a "lackey," call me a "clown," a "shop-assistant"—anything but a *shadchan*! But this new title of *shadchan* just tickled her to death—the widow, I mean. When she heard the word *shadchan* she just melted. "You'll be a mother-in-law soon," I tell her. But she smiles: "May I live to see it soon!" And what a mother-in-law she made! You should have seen her on her daughter's wedding-day. A feast for the eyes! A beauty! You would never say it was mother and daughter. Sisters—as I live! I couldn't tear my eyes away from her when the children stood under the canopy. "Ekh, you fool!" I said to myself. "You lonely old bachelor. Here is your opportunity. Just say the word, give one glance —and your lonely life is over. You make your own home. Cultivate your own vineyard. Enter your own Garden of Eden. You lead a quiet life among your near and dear ones. Forget Rosa, forget her! Rosa is not for you. You are old enough to be her father. Don't deceive yourself. Look at the mother. Tell her just one word, you goose! She's the one you should turn to! Make up your mind at last! Don't you see with what eyes she looks at you?"

Musing thus, I meet her glance, and pity for her smites my heart. Do you hear? Pity! Pity is all that now remains. I used to have quite a different feeling before, I remember. And now—only pity. And if pity—then maybe I, too, am to be pitied? And maybe more than her? Who then is to blame? Why had she kept silent all that time? Why is she silent now? Why should I have to tell her that word, and not she me? Ashamed, you say? It's the way of the world? A fat lot I care for your world! I don't see what difference it makes whether it's He first or She first. People are people. If she says nothing, I say nothing. You call it obstinacy? Pride? Folly? Call it what you like! I told you once before that I don't care a damn. I'm only telling you this so as to try with your help to analyze the whole thing and get to the bottom of it. Maybe the reason was that Paya and I never had two minutes together in private? There was always some living soul there to claim all our attention, time and feelings; our sorrows and joys—everything belonged to that other one, not to us. For ourselves we did not have a single spare minute. Damn it, we both seemed to have been made to take care of others! Before it was Pinye. Then, with God's help, Rosa was born, and now the Lord sent another joy—a son-in-law to keep! The son-in-law, however, was a real lucky find. Such a son-in-law anyone could wish himself. I don't have to tell you that I am not one of those who fall over themselves and I'm not in the habit of making a fuss of anybody. I'm not one for lavishing mealy-mouthed compliments, empty words, or crying up anybody. But let me tell you this—the word Angel in this case would have sounded like an insult. You follow me? If heaven exists, and if there are angels flying about in it, and if those angels are anything as good as that Shapiro, then all I say is it's worth while dying to be with them rather than with the two-legged animals who prowl about under God's skies and befoul the earth. You will say I am a misanthrope, a man-hater. If people did to you what they did to us, if they acted towards you as they acted towards us, you would be not a misanthrope, but a villain. You would go for people with a knife, kill them off like sheep! By the way, what's the idea of making a man speak for hours and not even asking him whether he wants a glass of water? Tell them to bring some tea please!

Let me see, where was I? Our new-found joy, our son-in-law Shapiro.

I believe I told you already that he was the head manager at the distillery, and not only the manager, but the absolute boss of the place. Everything was in his hands. The employers had absolute trust in him and loved him as if he were a son. At the wedding, his employers—two partners (a pair of double-dyed thieves—may they forgive me for saying so—who are now safe on the other side, in America)—bore themselves like near kinsmen. They gave the bridegroom a present of a box of silver things, and altogether were generous and kind, like real philanthropists. And I don't like philanthropists, you know, especially philanthropic employers who come to a party to show off their philanthropy so's everyone should see how a philanthropic employer can appreciate an employee! Maybe it was through that very employee that they had become rich? Maybe, if it hadn't been for that man, they would not have been employers nor philanthropists? You needn't smile. I'm not making myself out to be a Socialist, but if there is anyone I hate it is a philanthropic employer. Can you blame me? But wait, you haven't heard yet what a philanthropic employer is capable of doing. You'd think—now here's a man, who, with God's help, owns a factory that brings him in several thousand a year, and has in his service a man he can fully trust—well then, what better can he do than to sleep peacefully at home or go abroad and enjoy himself? But no, that is not enough! They like to do big business, to make a noise, so's everyone should see, everyone should hear! In a word, those thriving employers were not content with being the owners of a profitable concern which Shapiro ran successfully for them. They went in for new lines of business, got entangled in all kinds of jobbing and brokery, the purchase and sale of wheat, and bran, and finally houses. In a word, things hummed and roared and spun. The ground slipped from under their feet, and everything went up in smoke. They got our Shapiro mixed up in their shady affairs, left him with promissory notes on his hands, and themselves made off with all the cash to America. They seemed to be doing "all right" out there, as the Americans say, while he, Shapiro, was left up to the neck in debts, tied hand and foot with promissory notes and bills. In a word, there was a big bust-up, and things got so that no one cared whether he was an employee or an employer—let him meet the bills, and since he couldn't, then he was bankrupt. But he couldn't prove that this bankrupcy was not of his own doing. And such a man, as you know—or may not know—is considered with us a fraudulent bankrupt, that's to say a cheat, and such birds are put in prison, people here don't like them. You can go bankrupt ten times, do the trick ten times, but if you do it neatly and smartly you can get away with it and give the world the fig, and buy yourself a house with all the doodads into the bargain. You're an honest man again. Your children marry well, your opinion stands for something in the town, you give orders and boss the show, you make your way up in the world, aim at being one of the mighty of the earth, the big pots, who lead everyone by the nose. You begin to imagine you really are God knows who, you puff yourself up like a turkey-cock, you stop recognizing people in the street, and persuade yourself that you are a little tin God. Pardon me, but you understand that I don't mean you. But what's the use of talking? Shapiro could not face the shame of it, and, besides, his heart ached for the defrauded widows and orphans (his employers had spared no one, and had grabbed wherever they could), so he went and poisoned himself.

I don't think it matters to you how and what he poisoned himself with. And what letter he left me. And what he told me. And how he bade farewell to Rosa. And to her mother and me. All that is sentimental stuff which the novelists use to squeeze a tear out of the silly reader. To cut a long story short, it wasn't himself that that man poisoned—he poisoned us all! Our sorrow knew no bounds, the anguish of it was so deep that it dried up all our tears. We were stricken, turned to stone, we would have been the happiest of mortals if someone had come and chopped our heads off for us! Say what you like, but I hate all those people who express condolences. That hypocritical look of sorrow on their faces, on every one of which is written: "Thank God it isn't me...," their unfelt meaningless words, their false eulogies, their mutterings under the nose instead of the usual words at parting. That's nothing, though. Even the Book of Job, which it is a custom for every ignoramus to look into on such occasions, although he doesn't understand a damn about it—sickens me. Blasphemy, you say? In your opinion that's blasphemy? What about tripping up an absolutely innocent man, forcing him to sign promissory notes and then running off with the money to America, leaving a confidential agent in a hopeless plight and thereby driving him to commit suicide, leaving to the mercy of fate three innocent souls, ruining their lives—what would you call that? What name would you give that? Isn't that blasphemy? And the Lord God Himself, you will say, has nothing to do with it either. Because—how can you murmur at God? You just look what that same holy Job has to say about it in the book that people look into without understanding a word about it. You've got nothing to say? Nor have I. Because you can talk yourself hoarse, just the same no one will answer. You will go on chewing the same old words over and over again: "God giveth, God taketh" and much good may that do you. What do you say? Philosophizing is like chewing straw? That's just what I say.

Well then, coming back to the widow. . . . But what am I saying—the widow? My two widows. Rosa also is a widow. Ha, ha, ha! It's very sad, it's insulting, it's unnatural. But what is there left to do except laugh with a bitter laugh. Rosa—a widow! You should have seen her—a child of fifteen could not have looked younger! Rosa—a widow! But a widow is only half the story. Rosa is a mother! Rosa has a baby! Three months after Shapiro's death the voice of a new-born infant girl was heard. It filled the whole house. They called her Feigele, and Feigele it was who became the sovereign mistress of that house; whatever was done was done for Feigele, and wherever you stood, wherever you sat, whatever you did—all you heard was Feigele, Feigele, Feigele. If I were religious or believed in Providence, as you call it, I would say that the Most High had rewarded us for all our sufferings and sent us solace. But I'm not exactly religious, as you know, and I have strong doubts whether you are. What? You would have me believe that you are? All right, have it your way, I don't mind so long as you're convinced you are not a hypocrite and a pious fraud. I can't stand

47

hypocrites and pious frauds any more than a good Jew pork! Be as pious as ten thousand devils, only be honest about it! But if you're a hypocrite, a pious fraud who pretends to be a fanatic, then I have as much need of you as a cart of a fifth wheel! That's the kind of person I am.

Well, who was next on our list? Feigele! The very first minute that Feigele came into the world it became a brighter, happier, more joyous place. Faces glowed, eyes brightened and sparkled. We all seemed to have been born anew together with that child. Rosa, whose face had not worn a smile for so long, began to laugh again in her old infectious way that made you laugh even though you felt like crying.

That is what that tiny tot Feigele did to us when she opened her what we thought to be understanding eyes and began to examine the three of us. And when the first smile appeared on Feigele's lips, the two widows almost went crazy with delight.

They met me with such an outcry that I caught a fright.

"Good heavens! Where were you a minute ago?" the two widows fell upon me.

"Why? What's the matter?" I asked in alarm, and this is what I heard in reply:

"Why, only a minute and a half ago Feigele smiled for the first time!"

"Is that all?" I said rather coolly, while my own heart was glad, not so much, of course, that Feigele had smiled as that my two widows were so happy. I leave you to imagine what happened when she cut her first little tooth! The one to discover it first, naturally, was the younger widow, the mother. She called the older widow, that's to say Paya, and both of them began sounding the little girl's tooth carefully with the aid of a glass. And when they heard the glass tinkle against the tooth they raised such a noise that I rushed out of the next room more dead than alive.

"What's the matter?"

"A little tooth!"

"It's your imagination!" I said on purpose to tease them a bit. Thereupon the two widows took my finger and made me feel something that had a sharp edge to it in Feigele's hot little mouth.

"Well?" they both said, expectantly.

But I pretend to be puzzled. I love teasing them.

"Well what?" I ask.

"Isn't it a tooth?"

"What else could it be?"

And I don't have to tell you, of course, that once Feigele has cut a tooth, then she's the cleverest little girl and there isn't another like her in all the world. And once Feigele is so clever, then she has to be kissed until she starts crying. Then I tear her out of their hands and soothe the child, because no one is able to soothe a child quicker than I am, and for that matter Feigele loves no one's hair as she does mine, and there isn't a nose she more enjoys tweaking with her tiny fingers than mine. And the feel of those tiny fingers on your face is a sheer delight! You could kiss every little joint of those tiny velvety fingers a thousand times! You look at me and think, "That man is an old woman! Otherwise he wouldn't be so fond of children." I have guessed right, haven't I? I don't know whether I'm an old woman, but I do love children, that's a fact. Who are you going to love if not the little ones? The grown-ups? Those smooth well-fed mugs with paunches for whom life is a good dinner, a cigar, and a game of préférence? Or would you have me love those who feed on the community while they go about shouting and trumpeting to the world at large that their only aim is the public good? Or would you have me love those young cubs who are out to remake the world, who call me a "bourgeois," and want to make me sell my houses and share with them in the name of some expropriation or whatever they call it? Or would you have me love those well-fed ladies whose only ideal is to guzzle, dress themselves up in silks and diamonds, drag themselves round the theatres and make a hit with strange men? Or those bob-haired spinsters, who used to be called Nihilists and are now called *Esdekovki, Esserovki, Kodetki* and other such wonderful names? You say I'm a grumpy bachelor, a grouch, a misanthrope, and that's why I don't like anybody? So what? Is anyone the worse for it? Well, where did I leave off? The baby, Feigele, and how we all loved her. We gave our whole life to it, all three of us, because that child brought sunshine into our lives, gave us the strength and energy to bear the burdens of a gross and stupid existence. But for me that child was a source of secret hopes. You will readily understand what hopes if you remember what Rosa meant to me. The child grew up, and day by day the hope blossomed in my breast that my loneliness would end at last and that I, too, would some day taste the sweet of life. Nor was I the only one who lived in that hope. Paya, too, nourished that hope in her heart. And although we never spoke about it, it was as clear to us all as God's daylight that so it would be. I suppose you will ask—how can people understand each other without words? But that means that you know Psychology but you do not know human nature. Here, let me give you a picture, for instance, and you'll see how people can understand each other without a word.

A summer night. The sky is flecked with milk-white streaks. I was going to say—the stars are shining, twinkling, sparkling, but I remember having seen it in some book, and I don't like repeating someone else's words. I told you, I simply can't stand descriptions of nature which resemble nature as much as I do the Turkish pasha. In a word, it was a summer night, one of those surprisingly warm beautiful nights when the heart of even the most unfeeling man is filled with poetry, and the lure of distant places draws him. A great peace descends upon him, and he gazes into the overturned blue bowl called the sky, and feels that the sky and the earth are holding whispered converse with one another about eternity, about infinity, about what people call the godhead.

Well? How do you like my description of nature? You don't like it? Then don't! But wait, that's not all. I forgot to tell you about the beetles—those queer, heavy, flying beetles that buzz about in the dark, now hitting the wall or the window, now dropping on the ground with half-spread wings. Don't worry, they will crawl about over the ground a bit, then rise again, spread their wings and begin to fly around the light once more, buzzing and droning, to strike the window again, then drop to the ground. We sit on the doorstep out in the garden, all four of us—Paya, Rosa, Feigele and I. Feigele is already a big girl—she turned four last autumn—and speaks like a grown-up. Asking questions all the time. Thousands of questions! Why is the sky the sky, the earth the earth? When is day and when is night? Why is night night, and day day? Why does Mamma call Grandma Mamma, and Granny calls Mamma Rosa instead of Mamma? Why am I her uncle and not her papa? Why does Uncle look at Granny, and Granny at Mamma, and why does Mamma get so red? Everyone laughs at that. Feigele asks why we laugh, and we laugh still louder, and the end of it is that we three exchange glances and understand only too well what those glances mean. No words are needed. Words are useless. Words are for chatterboxes, for women and lawyers. Or, as Bismarck once said, words are given us to conceal our thoughts with. Take the birds, and the beasts and all the other creatures—they do without words! Trees grow, buds blossom, grass sprouts—what tongue have they? Eyes, my dear sir, human eyes—that's the thing! Eyes will sometimes tell you in one second what the tongue could not tell you in a day. The glances I and those two widows exchanged that night expressed a lot, such a lot.... Unforgettable glances—the poem of our lives, if you like, a song, the sad song of three wasted lives, of three maimed souls, whom the jogtrot, the hurly-burly of life had prevented from drinking at the fountain called Happiness, from tasting of the spring called Love. The word Love has escaped me unwittingly. The word, I tell you, makes me sick. Why? Because you writers use that sacred word too often, make it sound prosaic. The word Love in the mouths of you writers is a profanation. The word Love should sound like a prayer to the Almighty or like a melody without words, a song of pure poetry, even if it does not have rhymes like cry—buy, grab—nab, deal—steal and such-like, the reading of which makes me feel as if I were swallowing peas and washing them down with chewed paper. These comparisons of mine may not be to your liking, but have a little patience. I'll soon finish my story about widow number two, because if there's anything I can't stand it's to see someone yawning. Tell me, did you ever have this happen to you: your tooth hurts terribly, it has got to come out, but you keep putting off your visit to the dentist from day to day. At last you pluck up courage and go. On the dentist's door you read a sign: "Hours of attendance from 8 to 1 and from 1 to 8." You look at your watch and say to yourself: "From eight to one and from one to eight? Then what's the hurry?" And you go home and writhe in pain again. That's what happened with me and Rosa. Every morning I left the house firmly resolved to have it out with her. First I'll speak to widow number one, that's to say the mother. "So-and-so and so-and-so...." She will blush slightly, drop her eyes and say: "I have no objection, talk it over with Rosa." Then, from widow number one I go to widow number two and tell her: "Listen, Rosa, so-and-so and so-and-so...." And I go off to my widows, and out comes running Feigele, who rushes into my arms, throws her own round my neck, kisses my spectacles, and begs me to be sure and tell Mamma and Granny that very day—they always listen to me—that she should be allowed not to do her lessons, or to practise or dance, but to go to the Zoo with Uncle! They have new monkeys there, and they're so funny you can die with laughter! Well, you just try not to take the child to the Zoo to see the funny monkeys.

"What's going to come of that child?" grumbles widow number one.

"He'll spoil that child completely," chimes in widow number two.

But Uncle takes no notice of the chiding and reproaches of the two widows and goes off with the child to see the funny monkeys. And so every time some other reason. Day after day passes, week after week, year after year. The child grows, and begins to understand things that are not spoken of, and we three come to a tacit agreement to bide our time until the child grows up—we shall see when the time comes. When Feigele grows up and gets engaged, then we shall have our hands free to rearrange our lives and build our nest anew. And each makes plans on the secret how we are all going to live together: the young couple—Feigele and her husband, the old couple—I and Rosa, while the widow-grandma, Paya, will rule over us. That's the life! The thing is to live long enough to see Feigele grow up and find herself an affianced lover. But he who

lives long enough will live to see. That is how the saying goes, I believe? I don't like trite sayings, you
know. Do you? Ah well, you're welcome to it! Well
then, he who lives long enough will live to see. Feigele
grew up. When she was old enough she found herself
a *fiancé* and that's where the trouble begins. That's
where Psychology, as you call it, comes in.

You needn't look at the clock, I'm not going to tell
you any more today all the same. It's time I went. My
widows will be thinking God knows what. And if you
want to hear the story about widow number three, nothing will happen to you if you come round to my place.
I'm not pulling you by the skirts. If you want you'll
come. Good-bye!

So much for widow number two.

3

WIDOW NUMBER THREE

It's good you came just when I happen to be at home.
That is, I am always at home to myself, but not to others. Every man has his habits. Take me, for instance.
I'm used to having the cat sit opposite me when I am
eating. Without the cat I couldn't eat. Puss-puss-puss!
How do you like my pussy? Clever puss! She'll never
touch anything, not even if you left gold lying about.
And her fur! How do you like her fur? What? You don't
like cats? They put that idea into your head when you
were at *cheder*. Don't we know those tricks! You needn't
make excuses. Do you have tea with milk? Just plain?
I have mine with milk. Shoo! Go to the devil! There's
nothing she loves more than milk! She won't touch
butter, but she'll lap up milk like anything.

I'm no lover of introductions, as you know, but this
time there is no avoiding one. I hate when anyone
smiles. Laugh as much as you like, but please don't

smile. Do you remember everything I told you? Perhaps you have forgotten, don't be afraid to say so. Bigger men than you and I have had that happen to them. I'm afraid I'll have to run over it again briefly from the beginning.

I had a friend Pinye, he had a wife Paya, and they had a daughter Rosa. My friend died. Paya was left a widow. I was a near friend of hers. I liked her and she liked me. And so the best years of our life went by. Meanwhile Rosa, her daughter, grew up and I became fond of her. A young man turned up—Shapiro, a good bookkeeper and an excellent chess-player, and Rosa fell in love with him. Then I quarrelled with the mother and left the house intending never to return as long as I lived. I did not keep my word, and went back again the very next day. As before, I was an intimate friend of the family. We celebrated the wedding of Rosa and that Shapiro fellow, who ran the whole business on behalf of his principals and even signed bills for them. But they went to ruin and ran away to America, leaving him in debt. Shapiro committed suicide, and Rosa was left a widow. That gives us two widows. And like her mother Paya—widow number one—the daughter Rosa—widow number two—was left with a baby, Feigele, who was born three months after Shapiro's death. And we all loved the little girl, gave ourselves up to her entirely, so that we had no time to think of ourselves and our love for widow number two—that is, Rosa —an affair that had been dragging on for ever so long. We all thought: let Feigele grow up, become a big girl, and then we shall see. But when Feigele grew up and became a big girl.... Please don't look at your book when I am talking—it's a disgusting habit. I want you to listen carefully to what is coming, because this is the beginning of a new story.

You can think what you like of me, but I was never a fanatic or a bigot. I always kept in step with the age. I never lagged or pulled backwards like those who complain about the young generation with its modern tendencies.

I can't stand those old cleversticks with their perpetual pretensions: "Who's trying to teach the hen to lay eggs? Who's older—the egg or the hen?" Fools! The egg is all the more valuable for being the younger! It's more capable! Cleverer! And, of course, we, the old generation, should give heed to what the young people tell us, because they are young, and fresh, they study, they probe, they seek, they find, they discover. You can take it from me! You think they're like you—old snuff-and-pepper boxes, who sit poring over their musty old volumes and refuse to budge? To be sure, I am angry with the young folks, the modern generation, for not wanting to recognize us at all, for not caring a pin about us—listening to them, we're asses, and not even asses, but just nobody! Nothing! We don't exist! We're not there—and that's that! Just imagine, three young squirts come to us, that is, to our widows, or rather to Feigele. Students, not students—the devil knows what they are! Wear black blouses, don't cut their hair, who they are they don't say, tongues sharp as razors, and Karl Marx is their God—not the Prophet Moses even, but God Himself! Very well—God then God! You won't catch me laying hands on myself because of it. All the more that I lean a bit towards socialist ideals myself, and I don't have to be told what Capital is, the Proletariat, the Economic Struggle and all the rest of it. If you want to know, I'm a—You needn't rejoice, I'm not a Bundist, God forbid, but neither am I a lame tailor!

Well then, they came to us every day, those three chaps I'm telling you about. One was called Finkel, the other Bomstein and the third Gruzevich. And they felt quite at home at our place, because both my widows, the mother and the daughter, make such a fuss when anyone comes to visit them that they don't know where to seat the guest. Especially three such jewels, one of whom is undoubtedly a candidate for Feigele's hand. That is, all three are candidates, but Feigele can't very well have three *fiancés*. There must be one of them. Now go and guess who that one is, when you daren't even mention it, God forbid! They don't ask either. Who's there to ask? The mother? What do they want with the mother? A young woman with a beautiful face, that's all. The grandmother? What's the grandmother to them? The grandmother to them is just a housewife, whose duty it is to see that the guests have to eat and drink, and not just eat and drink, but eat and drink their fill. As for me, there's nothing to say. What am I to them? An extra chair at the table, nothing more. No one ever says a word to me. Unless it's to ask me to pass the salt, or the sugar or a match at the table—and even that's done without words, without even a "please"; just wave a hand at you as if you were a deaf-mute, or stick out a lip when you light a cigarette, that's all. Sometimes they find me alone. The three of them will then sit down and start a conversation among themselves. Not a word to me, not even for the sake of mere courtesy! You'd think I wasn't there. Well, I don't have to tell you that I wouldn't start a conversation with them for anything in the world. You won't catch me trying to make up to them like some people would and curry favour with words of flattery and fawning smiles. The man before whom I would humble myself has not yet been born. Not that I'm proud. And what if I were? Call me what you like—your opinion doesn't interest me! However, I hate to hear people talking about themselves. I'm telling you about those three whipper-snappers, what kind of birds they were.

One day I asked if any of them played chess. You should have seen their faces! You should have heard the way they laughed! You'd think—now what's wrong with chess? Can't a man be a socialist and play chess? I am sure Karl Marx would not have taken offence. That just shows you. But never mind them. It's Feigele who makes me angry. She laughs together with them. Why is it that everything they say is gospel truth to her, as if the Almighty Himself had uttered it on Mount Sinai? And what are these idols our modern youth have set up for themselves, what is this fanaticism—Karl Marx is our teacher, and we are his faithful followers. As if there isn't anyone else besides Karl Marx in the world? And where is Kant? Where is Spinoza, what's happened to Schopenhauer, where are Shakespeare, Heine, Schiller, Spencer and hundreds of other great men, who, too, may have let fall some clever word by accident? Not as wise, perhaps, as Karl Marx, but then they didn't exactly go about talking sheer nonsense either. I may as well tell you, I'm not one of those who lets anyone tread on his corns, and I don't like people putting on airs. In such cases I am sometimes purposely contra- dictory. You say this—I say that, and do your damned- est! One day I heard them saying that Count Tolstoi was a nobody. I'm not an ardent follower of Tolstoi's, no admirer of his philosophy and his latest teaching about Christ. But as an artist I wouldn't put Tolstoi be- low Shakespeare. You can agree with me or not, I don't care! You know me. Well, I purposely bring a book of Tolstoi's and give it to Feigele to read. You should have seen with what a grimace she pushed the book away! What's the matter? The matter is that neither Finkel, nor Bomstein, nor Gruzevich recognize Tolstoi.

This was more than I could stand (I can let myself go with a vengeance when I'm put to it, let me tell you) and I went for the three of them properly. `

Well, well! Did they flare up! If I had touched the holy of holies its followers would have taken it calmer than they did.

The two widows put a stop to the dispute, otherwise it would have ended in a serious row. Afterwards, however, I realized what a foolish thing I had done, because in the end I was only obliged to apologize to them. And do you know why? Because Feigele wanted me to. And when Feigele wants a thing she gets it. If she says, for instance, that I must move this house over to another place, it has got to be done and there must be no argument about it!

That girl has not only bewitched me, she has enslaved me, bent me to her will, turned me into a slave, a robot. And her marriage came as a surprise to all of us, and not only to me. The man of her choice was Gruzevich, a chemical student in his third year. Not a bad fellow; no genius, but otherwise he was all right. I've known worse. First of all he was from a respectable family. That means a lot. Say what you like, but there is something in that after all. Don't be afraid, I'm not going to talk about famousness. I'm just pointing out that descent counts in the long run too. If you are of doubtful origin, say from an ignorant family, then be you as educated as the Creator Himself, you'll always remain a churl. Of Gruzevich's other virtues I say nothing. Generally speaking, those boys, if the truth be told, are really honest, and decent, and noble so long as they keep true to themselves. But as soon as they make their way up in the world and become "somebody," you can't recognize them—those same "somebodies," are a thousand times worse than nobodies. Because a nobody, if he fools you, will try to clear out, whereas a "somebody," if he swindles you, will bring forward a thousand arguments to prove that it's you who are the swindler, not he.

But do not let us waste time in idle philosophy! Our Feigele became Mrs. Gruzevich at seventeen, and I will not stuff your head with the details of how the wedding went off and who arranged it, and how much it cost, and what rejoicing there was in our house. Mamma Rosa had lived to see her only daughter married, and Grandma Paya was happy to see her grand-daughter married. And I, fool that I am—What was I so glad about? That the youngest one had been married? The rejoicing, however, lasted only over Saturday and Sunday. On the third day after the wedding our Gruzevich was taken to the lock-up over some puddling affair: a store of bombs and dynamite had been discovered somewhere, and the lad being a chemist, and no mean chemist at that, the suspicion had fallen upon him. By the way, several letters of his had been found too. In a word, they ran him in.

This is when I got real busy, running about, moving heaven and earth, oiling palms. And all for nothing! Once you are caught red-handed, especially in a case like this, then it's good-bye! And to see the grief of seventeen-year-old Feigele! And the sufferings of her mother Rosa! And Grandma Paya! The wrath of God had descended upon this house. On top of it all, let me tell you, business started going bad, too. I was losing money, had to scheme and devise, mortgaged my houses. That money, too, went, and I had to sell my shops. I'm not trying to tell you how smart I was or to boast before you. I only want to show you what my widows were like. You'd think they'd at least take some interest in what they were living on, where the money came from, and what they were going to live on tomorrow. But they didn't care in the least! I had to see to everything! Think of everything! Exert all my energies! Who asked me to? Do I know? I'd like to see what you would do in my place with people about whom you could never decide which of them was the best? It was impossible to take offence at them, be angry or annoyed with them. And if a sense of injury did sometimes creep into your heart and you went home sulking, you only had to come again and meet those glances, hear their first word, for you to immediately forget that you had ever been annoyed with them. And again you were prepared to go through fire and water for their sake. That's the kind of creatures they are! What can you do? I say nothing about Feigele. That one draws you like a magnet. She just has to glance at you with her beautiful, deep, near-sighted eyes, and the devil has got your soul! Pardon me, I don't mean you, I'm saying this to myself, because that marriage of hers to Gruzevich absolutely drove me mad. Misha, they called him. And the house was full of him. No one spoke of anything else, no one cared for anybody else. No one could eat, no one could sleep, no one could live. What is it? Misha! They've taken Misha! They've arrested Misha! They're going to try Misha! Save Misha! But that's easier said than done. How were you going to save him? They didn't let anyone see him—neither me, nor her—no one. It was clear to me that things looked bad, that at best he was threatened with penal servitude for life, if not hanging. You are getting fidgety, I see. Come and sit over here, by the window. Or perhaps I'm boring you? Never mind. I've got more to bear than that. What is it to you? You'll hear out my story (I'm finishing soon) and go home, whereas to me it's a lifelong painful burden.

Now where were we? Yes, the verdict: he was sentenced to be hanged. No doubt you have often read in the papers that today, at such-and-such a place, two men have been hanged, and yesterday, at such-and-such a place—three. Hanging men these days is just like cutting chickens' throats for dinner. And what do you do meanwhile? You rock yourself in your chair and smoke an aromatic Havana, or drink a cup of tasty coffee with fresh rolls and butter. What is it to you that a man out there is swinging, twitching in his last throes, his death agony, a man near and dear, who not so long ago was full of life and strength, just as you are now? What is it to you that the body of a man whose life the executioners have taken lies out there still warm? That a man is going through hell out there, he wants to die quickly, but death doesn't come, because the hangman has tied the rope badly or the rope has broken under the weight of the body, and the man has dropped more dead than alive and pleads with dimming eyes for a speedy death? What? You don't like to be told such things? You are pampered. I am as pampered as you are. Yet I had been everywhere a man could be, and so I knew the exact minute and second when he would be executed, and afterwards I read in the papers that one of the three (they had hanged all three of them) had battled long with death, because he was a heavy man (that was Bomstein) and he had had to be hanged twice.... That's what they wrote afterwards in the newspapers, and we read it—not all of us, that is—only I and Rosa. We hid those papers from Grandma and grand-daughter.

Another young widow was added to the house—widow number three. And misery descended upon the house, a dumb deathly misery, which no words or paints can express. A misery which you cannot describe, for to describe it were to profane it. A misery which, depicted by any of you writers, would have sounded like blasphemy. A misery about which you cannot, must not, speak. Life was a load of dead aching memories. Three widows—three lives. Not full lives, but half-lives, or rather snatches, fragments of lives. Each had begun so well, so poetically—a brief flash, then all was gone. I say nothing about myself. I am not in it. That is, I go there every day, sit up with them night after night, and we talk about the happy days that have fled, we recapture old memories about my dear friend Pinye, about honest and noble Shapiro, about Misha Gruzevich, of whom the papers afterwards wrote that in his field, in chemistry, he was a genius. I leave them every day with an aching heart and ask myself with annoyance why I have so foolishly wasted my life. When and where had I made my first mistake, and when would I make my last? I love all three of them, and all three are dear to me, and any one of them might have been mine, and might still be.... And to all three of them I am a dear and a nuisance, I am wanted and unwanted. If I miss a day and do not come there is a row, and if I stay half an hour longer I am sent packing, simply told to clear out. They do nothing without asking me, but if I reproach them for anything, they say I am meddlesome. I lose my temper, run home, and lock myself up with my cat, and tell the servant that if anyone calls, I am not at home, I have gone away. I take up my diary again, which I have been keeping for thirty-six years without a break. It's an interesting diary, you may be sure. I am keeping it for myself, not for others. Your literature will have a long time to wait before it gets a book like that. I'll show it to you one day, maybe, but I won't show it to anyone else, not for anything in the world.

But hardly half an hour passes when someone knocks on my door.

Who's that? A maid from the widows calling you to dinner. What shall I tell her? Tell her I am coming in a minute.

Well, what do you say now, my dear sir? How about that Psychology of yours? You're in a hurry to go? Come along, I'll go with you. I have to go and see my three widows. Just a minute, I'll tell the servant to feed the cat—I may sit there till the morning for all I know. We play *yeralash,* sometimes préférence. We play for money. Each one is eager to win. If anyone makes a blunder, no mercy is shown him—whether it's me or them. Every wrong lead, when we play cards, makes me furious, I'm ready to murder the bungler.

What does that smile of yours mean? Believe me, I know what you're thinking just now. I can see right through you. But I don't care a hang. You're thinking: "You old, grumpy bachelor...."

Well, that's the whole story about the three widows.

1907

THE BEWITCHED TAILOR

(From an Old Chronicle)

Chapter One

THERE dwelt a man in Zlodeyevka, a small town in the district of Mazepovka, not far from Khaplapovich and Kozodoyevka, between Yampol and Strishch, on the road that runs from Pishi-Yabeda through Pechi-Khvost to Teterevets and thence to Yegupets.

And the name of that man was Shimen-Eli, but he was called Shimen-Eli *Shma-Koleinu*, because of the spirited way he prayed in the synagogue, where he would shout, roll up his eyes, snap his fingers, and troll away for all he was worth.

And that man was a tailor—not, God forbid, one of your high-class tailors, who sew from the "pictures" called "fashion books," but just a master of the mending craft, that is, one who had no rival in making a patch, or darning a hole so neatly that you could never tell it had been done, or turning a garment, no matter how old, inside out, and making it look exactly like new. He would take, for instance, an old capote and make a gaberdine out of it, and out of the gaberdine a pair of trousers, out of the trousers he'd carve a waistcoat, and out of the waistcoat something else again. And that is no easy job, I don't mind telling you!

But Shimen-Eli *Shma-Koleinu* was very smart at it. And Zlodeyevka being a poor little town where the making of new clothes was not what you would call a regular habit with people, Shimen-Eli was held in great esteem. The only trouble with him was that he could not get along with the rich men of the town. He liked to poke his nose into community affairs, to interfere on behalf of the poor, and speak his mind rather openly about the philanthropists, who were supposed to have the public interests at heart; the *baltakse*, for instance, he just dragged through the mud, calling him in front of everybody an extortioner, a blood-sucker, and a cannibal, and the rabbis and the *shochtim*, who were at one with him, just a gang of thieves, swindlers, cut-throats, robbers, and scoundrels—the devil take them all together with their fathers, and their grandfathers, and their great-grandfathers right back to old fogey Terech, with Uncle Ishmael—the Turk—thrown in for good measure!

Among his fellow-craftsmen of the "Devout Toiler" fraternity, Shimen-Eli had the reputation of being a "musician." In their idiom this meant a person who was well up in his letters, for Shimen-Eli was always spouting maxims and quoting from the Talmud and other holy writings, such as: "Thy most unworthy," "Rejoice and be merry," "Today the world trembles," "The lowly and the downtrodden," "For it is written," inserting in and out of place Hebrew words and sayings which always came readily to his tongue. In addition, he had not a bad voice, if it was rather shrill and squeaky. But then he had all the synagogue chants and prayers at his finger-tips, loved to sing the service, was the *gabai* of the tailors' *shool*, and, as the custom was, got a good hiding at *Simchas Torah*.

Although Shimen-Eli had been wretchedly poor all his life—almost a beggar, you might say—he always tried to look on the bright side of things.

"On the contrary," he used to say, "the poorer the merrier, the hungrier I am the louder I sing! As it says in the Good Book, 'It becometh Israel to be poor as it becometh the beauteous maid Khivrya to wear stylish shoes. . . .'"

To make a long story short, Shimen-Eli was one of those of whom it is said, "A poor bird but a gay one." He was a scraggy little man with a skimpy goatee, a slightly flattened nose, a harelip, and large black eyes that never stopped smiling. He always had bits of fluff sticking in his curly hair, and his coat was like a pin-cushion. He walked with a dancing gait, forever humming to himself, "Today is *Yom Kippur* when the world trembles—so cheer up!"

Now Shimen-Eli was blessed with a large family. He had a houseful of children, mostly daughters, among whom were several grown-up girls. And he had a wife named Tsipe-Beile-Reize, who was the exact opposite of her husband: a tall, blooming, robust Cossack of a woman. The very day after the wedding she took him in hand and had never let go since. She ruled the roost, and at home it was she, really, and not he, who was the man of the house. Her husband stood in trembling awe of her. He would begin to tremble as soon as she opened her mouth. There were times—no one being there to see it—when she treated him to a resounding slap in the face. Shimen-Eli would put it in his pocket and laugh the matter away with a joke or his favourite saying: "Today the world trembles—so cheer up! As the scripture says, 'And he'—that is, the husband—'shall rule over thee. . . .' So there you are!

And all the kings of East and West can do nothing about it."

And there came a day one summer when Tsipe-Beile-Reize returned from the market with her shopping-bag in her hand, threw down the bunch of garlic, the parsnips and potatoes that she had bought, and cried out in anger: "May it all sink into the earth! I'm sick and tired of it all. Day in day out I suck my brains dry, thinking what to make for dinner! You need the head of a minister on your shoulders! Dumplings and beans, beans and dumplings—that's all we know, may God forgive us! Now look at Nechame-Broche. There's beggar if ever there was one, a miserable *Kabtzen*—and even she has a goat! And why? Because her husband, Leizer-Shloime, is a man, even though he *is* a tailor! Just think of it—a goat! With a goat in the house, you always have a glass of milk for the children; if you like you can cook *kasha* with milk, make shift with dinner, with supper, sometimes a jug of buttermilk, some cottage cheese, some butter. It's a pleasure!"

"You are right, my dear," Shimen-Eli answered mildly. "It stands written even in the *Medresh*: 'Unto every Israelite is given his share,' that is to say, every Jew must have his goat.* As it says in the scripture—"

"What do I want with your scripture!" Tsipe-Beile-Reize shouted. "You tell him goat and he tells you scripture! I'll give you such a scripture that it'll turn dark in your eyes! He feeds me with scripture, my feeder, my blessed *shlimazl*! I wouldn't give one decent dairy *borshch* for all your learning, do you hear!"

And Tsipe-Beile-Reize began to nag her husband and drop hints like these several times a day, until, at last, he repented him and swore that she could sleep in peace

* One of Shimen-Eli's usual misquotations. The Talmudic text reads: "Unto every Israelite is given his share of the Kingdom of Heaven."—*Tr.*

68

from now on. With God's help, there would be a goat! The thing was not to lose hope. "Today the world trembles— so cheer up!"

From that day Shimen-Eli began to save up, kopek by kopek. He denied himself many things, even the common necessaries of life, pawned his Sabbath gaberdine, and so managed to scrape together a few rubles. It was decided that he was to take the money and go with it to Kozo-doyevka to buy a goat. Why to Kozodoyevka? For two reasons: in the first place because Kozodoyevka, as its name implies,* was a place where they kept goats. Secondly, Tsipe-Beile-Reize had heard say that a neighbour of hers whom she had not been on speaking terms with for some years, had heard from her sister, who lived in Kozodoyevka and had recently come to visit her, that there was a *melamed*—a Hebrew teacher—living there, who had been nicknamed Chaim-Chone the Wise, because he was such a fool; and that that *melamed* had a wife named Teme-Gittel the Silent, because she talked nineteen to the dozen; and that Teme-Gittel the Silent had two goats, both of them milkers. Now, I ask you: what does she want with two goats, and both of them milkers at that? She might not have had even one—there's nothing terrible in that! There are some Jews—bless the Lord—who don't have even half a goat. So what? Do they die from it?"

"You are quite right," answered Shimen-Eli. "It's an old story, you know.... It stands written: 'Askakoordi, debarbanti....'"**

"Again? Again he's here with his scripture!" his wife interrupted him. "You talk to him about a goat, and he comes at you with his scripture! Better go to that *melam-ed* in Kozodoyevka and tell him: well, so-and-so and so-and-so, this is how it is. We heard that you have two goats,

* The name in Russain literally means "Goat-Milker".—*Tr.*
** Gibberish, made to sound the language of the Talmud.— *Tr.*

69

both of them milkers. What do you want two milking goats for? It's ridiculous! And if that's the case, then you must be wanting to sell one of them, I am sure? Well, then, sell it to me! What difference does it make to you? Tell him just what I'm telling you, you understand?"

"Do I understand? What is there to understand?" said Shimen-Eli. "For my own money must I beg? Money can get you anything in the world. 'Silver and gold doth cleanse even pigs.' It's worse when you have no *gelt* at all. That's when you really can say, 'A poor man is as good as a dead man,' which is as much as to say, 'When there's nothing to eat, go bye-bye,' or, as the saying goes, 'You can't thumb a nose if you haven't got fingers.' There is another maxim that says, 'Askakoordi, debarbanti, de-farshmachti. . . .' "

"Again the books! Again scriptures! My head is splitting from your scriptures, may you sink into the earth with them!" retorted Tsipe-Beile-Reize, and once more she began to nag her husband, telling him for the hundredth time to go and try his luck with *melamed* Chaim-Chone, maybe something would come of it. And what if he didn't want to sell it? But why shouldn't he want to? Why should he have two goats, both of them milkers? There are still Jews in the world—bless the Lord—who don't have even half a goat. So what? Do they die from it?

And so on in the same vein.

Chapter Two

And when it was light, our tailor arose betimes, said his prayers, took his staff and his girdle, and footed it.

It was Sunday, a bright summer day. Shimen-Eli could not remember when he had seen such a fine day upon God's earth. It was a long time since Shimen-Eli had been out in the field in the open air. It was a long time since his eyes had seen such a fresh green forest, such a beautiful green carpet patterned with gay flowers. It was long since he had last heard the twitter of birds and the flutter of wings, long since his nose had sniffed the delightful smells of green grass and damp earth.

It was in quite a different world that Shimen-Eli *Shma-Koleinu* had spent his whole life. It was upon entirely different scenes that his eyes had gazed: a gloomy basement with a stove near the door and around it—oven forks, pokers, shovels, and a slop-pail full to the brim; next to the stove and the slop-pail—a bed of three boards; on the bed—children, a lot of children, God bless them, one smaller than the other, and all half-naked, barefoot, unwashed, forever hungry. To the ears of Shimen-Eli had come other sounds—voices crying, "Mamma, bread! Mamma, I want to eat! I'm hungry!" And drowning all these voices, the voice of Tsipe-Beile-Reize: "You want to eat? May the worms not eat you, O Merciful God, together with our dear *schlimazl* of a father! May the devils not take you together with him!" The nose of Shimen-Eli was accustomed to other odours: the smell of damp walls, dripping wet in the winter, green with mould in the summer; the smell of sour dough and bran, of onions and cabbages, of wet plaster, gutted fish and entrails; the reek of old clothes steaming under the hot iron.

And now, having escaped for a moment from that drab squalid world into the bright sunshine and freedom, our Shimen-Eli felt like a man who plunges into the sea upon a hot summer day: the waves bear him along, drive him onward, he dives again and again, and comes up to fill his lungs with the fresh air. What bliss, what a paradise on earth!

"Now, what would God lose," he thought, "what would God lose if every workingman, say, were given a chance to come out here into the fields every day, or at least once a week, to revel in the joys of God's lovely world? Ah, what a world! Is it not beautiful!"

And Shimen-Eli, as was his wont, began to hum prayers, which he refashioned in his own way. "O Lord, Thou hast created this Universe, this ancient world of Thine, outside the town. Thou hast chosen us and ordained that we, Thy Jews, shall live in Zlodeyevka, herded together in crowded stuffy dwellings. And Thou didst give us, O Lord, woes and worries, poverty, boils, and body-aches, in Thy boundless mercy, bim, bim, bom...."

Thus sang Shimen-Eli to himself, and he wanted to throw himself down upon the grass right where he stood, to forget the world and its cares if only for a moment, and taste the sweet of life. But he had an urgent errand to attend to, he reminded himself, and said, "Stop that now, Shimen-Eli! Enough singing, Shimen-Eli! Push along, brother, push along! You will rest, please God, at Oak Inn. The keeper there, Dudi, is a kinsman of yours after all, a blood relation. There, any time you please, you can toss your glass. For it is written that 'the study of the *Torah* comes before all else,' hence—'a drop of you know what is the most important thing of all'."

And Shimen-Eli *Shma-Koleinu* proceeded on his way.

Chapter Three

At the roadside, exactly midway between Zlodeyevka and Kozodoyevka, stands the country tavern known as Oak Inn. This inn has a strange attractive power, which, like a magnet, draws to itself both the *balagula* and his passengers going from Zlodeyevka to Kozodoyevka, or returning from Kozodoyevka to Zlodeyevka. None of them has ever been able to pass Oak Inn without stopping there if only for a few minutes. The secret of this attraction has yet to be discovered. Some say it is because the innkeeper, Dudi, is a most amiable and hospitable fellow, that is to say, he will always give you for your money a goodly glass of vodka and the best of snacks to go with it; others say it is because Dudi is supposed to be one of those who are called "prophets" or "guessers," which means that although he does not deal in stolen goods himself, he is on familiar terms with all the famous thieves. But as no one really knows this for sure, we had better say no more about it.

This Dudi was a hulking hairy fellow with a big belly and a potato nose, and he did not speak—he roared like a bull. He made a very comfortable living, had several cows, and everything a man could want. The only thing he didn't have, as the saying goes, was a headache. He was left a widower in his old age. He was an ignorant man without any learning and to him the women's prayer-book, the Passover service, or the Grace—were all one. That was why Shimen-Eli, the tailor, was ashamed of his kinship with him: it did not become him, a learned man and *gabai* of his synagogue, to have such a lubberly and ignorant tavern-keeper of a relative. And Dudi, for his part, was ashamed to have such a poor man and a tailor at that for a relative. Taking one thing with another, there was no love lost between them.

And yet, when Dudi caught sight of the tailor, he greeted him quite nicely, not because he respected his kinsman, but because he was a little afraid, if you ask me, not of his kinsman but of his kinsman's tongue.

"Oh!" he cried. "A guest! What a guest! How are you, Shimen-Eli? How is your Tsipe-Beile-Reize? How are the children?"

"Ah, 'What are we, what is our life?'" Shimen-Eli answered, as was his wont, with a quotation. "You know the saying: 'Some perish from the fire, others from the plague.' If it's not one, it's the other. The thing is to keep well. As it is written: 'Askakoordi, debarbanti, defarshmachti, dekoornosi...' How are you getting on, my dear kinsman? What is new here, out in the country? 'The fish we shall aye remember'—I still remember the *vareniki* and the drinks you treated me to last year. That's all that matters to you. You are no lover of looking into the books, I know. 'And why do the peoples mutter in vain?'—but what do you care for the Holy Word? Ah, Reb Dudi, Reb Dudi! If your father, my uncle Gdale-Wolff—may his soul rest in peace!—were to get up from his grave and take a look at his Dudi, see him living in the country among the ignorant, he would die a second time. Ah, what a father you had, Reb Dudi! A good Jew—may he forgive me for saying so—he drank like a fish. 'Remember the wormwood and the gall'—no matter what you talk about, your thoughts always turn to death. Ah, well, give me a glass; as our wise teacher Reb Pimpom* says, 'Pawn thy shirt and get thyself a drink!'"

"At it already? Spouting the scriptures again?" said Dudi, placing a glass of vodka before him. "Tell me first, Shimen-Eli, where are you travelling to?"

"I am not travelling," answered Shimen-Eli, tossing off the glass, "I am walking. As we say in our prayers, 'They have legs and they walk not,' that is, if you have legs there is no harm in using them."

"In that case," said Dudi, "tell me, dear heart, where are you walking to?"

"I am walking," said Shimen-Eli, draining his second glass, "to Kozodoyevka to buy goats. For it is written: 'Thou shalt create thyself goats'—buy goats, that is."

"Goats?" Dudi said in surprise. "Since when have tailors started to deal in goats?"

"Did I say 'goats'? I mean only one goat," explained Shimen-Eli. "Maybe, with God's help, I'll be able to buy a

* A fictitious personage.—*Tr.*

74

cheap goat somewhere—a *metsiah*. Not that I really want to buy one myself, only my wife Tsipe-Beile-Reize—God bless her!—has set her heart on it. You know what she is, once she has made up her mind. Screams, I want a goat! And a wife has to be obeyed, you say. It says so in the Talmud, too. You remember, don't you?"

"You understand these things better than I do," said Dudi. "You know very well that I'm not well up in the —what d'you call it—*Medresh*. There's one thing I can't make out, though, my dear kinsman—how come you to know all about goats?"

"I like that!" Shimen-Eli said, nettled. "What does an innkeeper know about prayers? Yet, when Passover comes, you gabble through the *Yom Kippur* service and somehow get away with it with God's help, don't you?"

The shot went home. Dudi bit his lip and said to himself: "You wait, you miserable stitcher! You've got a lot to say for yourself today! Trying to show off how learned you are! I'll show you goats—you wait!"

And Shimen-Eli demanded for himself another glass of that strong brew that cures all human ills. If the truth must be told, Shimen-Eli loved his glass. But a drunkard he was not. God forbid! Indeed, when could he allow himself the luxury? The trouble with him was that when he took one drink he could not deny himself another. And after two drinks his spirits soared immediately, his cheeks flushed, his eyes sparkled, and his tongue—his tongue loosened and ran away with him.

"Speaking of guilds," began Shimen-Eli, "we work-people of the Shears and Iron have one thing in common: we all like honours. And honours, they say, is something you've got to earn. The meanest cobbler wants to be somebody, the first *gabai*, if only over the slop-pail. I tell them: 'Friends,' I tell them, 'I am unworthy of your favours'—who the devil wants it! Elect a shoemaker your *gabai*. 'I want neither thy honey nor thy sting. Keep your honours and the kicks that go with them.' And they say, 'Kicks you will get, but *gabai* you shall remain.' But there! You are keeping me here, talking, and I have quite forgotten that I have a goat on me. The day stands not still. Good-bye, Reb Dudi, let us take heart! Keep well and cook your *vareniki*!"

"Now mind you don't forget and stop here on your way back," said the innkeeper.

"If God wills it!' answered Shimen-Eli. "I don't promise, but I'll try. Why, certainly, of course! We are only human, flesh and blood, as they say. Have a good glass of vodka on hand with a bite of something to eat, as befits us work-people of the Shears and Iron!"

Chapter Four

And Shimen-Eli departed from Oak Inn in the best of humours and slightly in his cups, and arrived safe and sound in Kozodoyevka. Upon arriving there he began to make inquiries where he could find the *melamed* Chaim-Chone the Wise, who had a wife named Teme-Gittel the Silent and two milking goats.

He did not have long to ask, for Kozodoyevka, please God, is not such a vast city that one is likely to lose one's way in it. The whole place lies spread before the eyes, with its butcher shops and its butchers, its meat choppers and its market dogs; with its market-place where the housewives, in stockinged shoeless feet, rush about from one peasant woman to another, all pulling and pinching the same chicken together.

"Listen, how much do you want for that hen?"

"What hen? It ain't a hen, it's a cock."

"Let it be a cock. What do you want for the hen?"

A couple of paces away is the synagogue yard. Old women sit there, selling small pears, sunflower seeds and beans. Right there the *melameds* hold their classes. The children shout, the goats—there are no end of goats!—skip about, nibble the straw off the roofs, or sit on the ground, wagging ginger little beards, sunning themselves and chewing the cud.

And over there is the bath-house, its walls black with soot. Next to it is a little stream covered with green scum and swarming with leeches and croaking frogs. The stream sparkles in the sun with all the colours of the rainbow and smells to high heaven.

And on the other side of the stream is nothing but earth and sky—that is where Kozodoyevka ends.

Reb Chaim-Ohone the Wise was at work when the tailor found him. In a *tallis-kot'n* and skull-cap, he was sitting with his pupils, leading them in a loud singsong recitation of a Talmudic treatise: "And the said goat, perceiving that there was food on the top of the barrel, did go after it ravenously...." Shimen-Eli *Shma-Koleinu* rattled off an abstruse bit of greeting in Aramaic, which he there and then translated into the vernacular: "May a good day burst upon you and your pupils, dear Rabbi. I hear you are discussing the very thing for which I have taken the trouble to come and see your good wife, Madame Teme-Gittel—that's to say about the goat. Not that I want to buy a goat really, but my wife Tsipe-Beile-Reize—God bless her!—is set on having one. Screams, I want a goat! And a wife, as you know, has to be obeyed. For it stands written in black and white: 'Askakoordi, debarbanti, defarshmachti, dekoornosi....' What are you staring at me like that for? 'Look not into the glass, look into the bottle'—never mind that I am just a common tailor Jew. 'Happy are ye who toil with your hands!' I daresay you have heard about me. I am Shimen-Eli, the tailor, from the holy city of Zlodeyevka, guild member and *gabai* of the synagogue, although, who the devil wants it! 'I want neither thy honey nor thy sting.' Keep your honours, I told them, and the kicks that go with them. And they say, 'Kicks you will get, but *gabai* you shall remain.' But here I am talking and have almost forgotten to greet you. Peace unto you, Rabbi. Peace unto you, children, holy lambs, holy terrors, imps of mischief! If you only studied as much as you now want to play! Have I guessed right?"

Hearing these speeches, the boys began to pinch one another on the sly, and sputtered and choked with laughter. They were delighted at the interruption and would fain have such visitors come every day. But Chaim-Chone the Wise did not share his pupils' glad feelings. He did not like to be interrupted in his work. So he called his wife, Teme-Gittel, and going back with his pupils to the goat which had got hold of the food on the barrel, began chanting at the top of his voice: "And the Rabbi decreed that the goat must fully compensate the damage, and pay for both the food and the barrel...."

Seeing that there was no use talking to the *melamed*, Shimen-Eli tackled his wife. And so while her husband and his pupils were busy with the Talmudic goat, Shimen-Eli discussed her own goat with Teme-Gittel.

"As you see, I am a plain tailor Jew," he declared. "You may have heard of me. I am Shimen-Eli, the tailor, from the town of Zlodeyevka, member of the Shears and Iron and *gabai* of the tailors' synagogue.... Although, who the devil wants it! 'I want neither thy honey nor thy sting.' Keep your honours, I told them, and the kicks that go with them. Well then, I have come to see you about one of your goats. Not that I really want to buy a goat, but my wife Tsipe-Beile-Reize—God bless her!—is set on having one. Screams, I want a goat! What can you do? A wife has to be obeyed, you know. It says so in the Talmud, black and white...."

Teme-Gittel, a little woman with a bean of a nose, which she kept wiping with two fingers, listened until she could listen no more, then interrupted:

"So you have come to buy one of my goats? Well, my dear man, I might as well tell you: for one thing—I don't intend to sell my goat. Because, speaking frankly —why should I? For the sake of money? What is money? Money rolls. Money goes, but a goat remains a goat. Especially a goat like mine. A goat, did I say? She's a mother, I tell you, not a goat! So easy to milk, touch wood! And the amount of milk she gives! And what does she eat? Call that eating? A mash of bran once a day, and for the rest the straw off the synagogue roof. Still, if you offered me a good price, I might think it over. Money, as you say, is tempting, and for money I could buy myself another goat—although I'll hardly find another as good as mine. A goat, did I say? She's a mother, not a goat! But what's the use of talking. I'll bring the goat in and you'll see for yourself."

Teme-Gittel ran out and came back at once with the goat and a full crock of milk which the goat had given that day.

When he saw that milk the tailor licked his lips and said:

"Tell me, my dear woman, what is she worth to you? I mean, how much do you want for this goat of yours? If the price is not a reasonable one, I won't buy it. Shall I tell you why? Because I need it like a cart a fifth wheel. The trouble is that my wife, that's to say, Tsipe-Beile-Reize—God bless her!—is set on having one. She screams—"

"What do you mean—how much?" Teme-Gittel broke in, wiping her little nose. "Name your price, let's hear it. Let me tell you one thing, though. No matter what price you pay you'll be getting a bargain. Do you know why? Because if you buy my goat you will have a *goat....*"

"Well, I like that!"—this time the tailor interrupted. "That's what I am buying her for, because she's a goat and not a blessed dummy! Not that I really want to buy her, because I need it as much as a dog a ticket-pocket. Only my wife, that is, Tsipe-Beile-Reize—God bless her! —is set on having one. She screams—"

"That's just what I was saying," Teme-Gittel started off again without waiting to hear the rest, and began going over all the points of her goat once more.

But the tailor did not let her finish. They kept interrupting each other until they both fell to speaking at once, and the result was a mishmash something like this: "A goat, did I say? She's a mother, not a goat!" "Not that I want to buy—" "A mash of bran—" "But she was set on having one—" "Money rolls, you know—" "And how easy she is to milk, touch wood!" "That is, Tsipe-Beile-Reize—" "Once a day ... straw off the roof—" "She screams—" "A wife has to be obeyed—" "A goat? She's a mother, not a goat!"

At this point Chaim-Chone the Wise broke in with: "Haven't you talked goats enough? Who ever heard of such a thing? People here are busy studying, and all they know is goats this, goats that, goats here, goats there! One of the two: either sell him the goat, or don't sell him the goat! It's all I hear: goats, goats! My head is full of goats!"

"Quite right!" answered Shimen-Eli. "Where there is learning there is wisdom. One of the two, what's the use of wasting breath? 'I have the silver, I have the gold.' I have the money, you have the goods. So let's strike a bargain. As it says in the prayer—"

"What do I want with your prayers? Tell me how much are you willing to give for the goat?" Teme-Gittel said, sinking her voice to a whisper and wiping her lips, while she arched herself like a cat.

"Well, I like that!" Shimen-Eli answered in the same low voice. "What do you mean—tell me? What am I—a story-teller or something? No, I have given myself trouble for nothing, I see. I shall not buy a goat today. Sorry to have troubled you...."

And turning towards the door, Shimen-Eli made as if to go.

"What's the matter with you, man!" cried Teme-Gittel, catching the tailor by the sleeve. "What's the hurry? Has a river caught fire? If I am not mistaken you were saying something about a goat...."

To cut a long story short, Teme-Gittel named her price, and the tailor named his; at last, after a good deal of haggling—a thousand less, a thousand more—they came to terms. Shimen-Eli counted out the money, and, taking off his girdle, tied it round the goat's neck. Teme-Gittel spat on the money for luck, wished the tailor joy and saw him out with many whisperings and glances at the money in her hand.

"Go in good health, and keep in good health, and enjoy good health, and, please God, it should be the same with you it has been till now—no worse—may you have everything of the best without end! And may she live with you and live with you, and give milk without a stop...."

"Amen! The same to you!" the tailor answered, making for the door.

But the goat refused to go. She shook her horns, sat down on her haunches, and bleated like a young cantor trying his voice in the synagogue for the first time. "Le-e-e-eave me alone! Wha-a-at have I done?" As much as to say, "Where are you dragging me?"

But Chaim-Chone the Wise arose in person and helped to drive the goat out of the house with his rod, while his pupils lifted their voices, shouting, "Goat! Goat! Get out, goat!"

And the tailor proceeded on his way.

Chapter Five

And the goat did resist—that is, she did not want to go to Zlodeyevka with the tailor, not for anything in the world. She struggled with all her might to go back. But it was no use. Shimen-Eli dragged her along by the halter, explaining to her the futility of all her efforts. Neither kicking nor bleating would help her.

"It is written in our holy books," he said to the goat, " 'against thy will art thou alive.' Of necessity must thou bear thy exile. No one asks you. I, too, was once a free bird—may I be forgiven for saying so—as fine a lad as anyone, with a fancy waistcoat and boots that squeaked. What more did I need? A headache? But the Lord said unto me, 'Go forth from thy land'—crawl into the sack, Shimen-Eli. Marry Tsipe-Beile-Reize. Beget children. Bear trials and tribulations all thy life long. 'For that is thy destined lot.' For what art thou but a tailor?"

Thus spake Shimen-Eli to the goat as he strode along almost at a run. A balmy breeze fluttered the skirts of his patched gaberdine, stole under his side ringlets, stroked his little beard, and wafted to his nose the spicy odours of mint, camomile and other wild flowers whose scents the tailor had never smelt before.

Enraptured, he began to read the afternoon prayer— that part of it which speaks of "balsam, incense, sweet-scented myrrh" and sundry other gums and spices. He read it in a singsong voice, exactly as he did in the synagogue on a holiday. He was wound up to chant through the whole service, when suddenly, what should come flying up but an evil tempting spirit, whispering these words into the tailor's ear:

"Look here, you silly fool, you! What are you singing for on an empty stomach? It will soon be night, and you haven't had a thing in your mouth all day, except those two small glasses of vodka. Besides, didn't you give your kinsman your word that on your way back with the goat you would drop in and have a bite with him? If you have given your word—keep it! A tongue is not a broom!"

And Shimen-Eli finished his prayers in a hurry and turned into the tavern as blithe as a bird.

"Good-evening, dear kinsman, Reb Dudi. I have good news to tell you. Congratulate me—I have bought a goat after all. And what a goat! A goat of goats! A goat our forefathers never dreamt of. Take a look at her and tell me what you think—after all, you are a learned man. How much should I have paid for her?"

Dudi screened his eyes against the sun, which was dipping beyond the gilded edge of the sky, examined the goat with the air of a connoisseur and valued it at exactly double the price the tailor had paid for it. This tickled Shimen-Eli so much that he let himself go to the extent of slapping the innkeeper on the back.

"Reb Dudi, my heart! May your health increase! 'Thy words are just'—this time you have guessed wrong. May we both have as many happy years."

Dudi pursed his lips, shook his head and grunted, "Foo, foo, foo!" as much as to say, "A bargain! You couldn't have got it cheaper if you had stolen it!"

Shimen-Eli, in his turn, cocked his head to one side and hooked his thumb through the armhole of his vest, as if he were going to pull a needle out and start threading it.

"Well, Reb Dudi? What do you say now, man of the people? Does this Jew know how to do business or not? You ought to see how much milk she gives—you'd drop down dead where you stand!"

"May you drop down dead yourself!" retorted Dudi.

"Amen! The same to you!" said Shimen-Eli. "And now, if I *am* such a welcome guest, take my goat, please, and fix her up somewhere in the barn, so's no one should steal her—God forbid! Meanwhile, I'll rattle off the eve-

ning prayer—I've done with the afternoon one on the way
—and then we'll put away a little glass and have a bite.
As it stands written in the holy books: 'No dance goes
before food.' Does that stand written, Reb Dudi, or does
it not?"

"What a question? Once you say it does, it does. You
are the learned one."

His devotions over, the tailor said to Dudi, "Well, if
it's as bad as that, then 'satisfy my hunger,' and my
thirst too, while you're at it. Pour a drop out of that
little green bottle and let's drink to our healths, dear
kinsman. Health first, you know! As we say every day in
our prayers, 'Return us in peace.'"

After a drink and a bite or two our tailor let himself
go with a vengeance on the subject of Zlodeyevka, of
the local community, of synagogical affairs, of the guild
and the tailoring trade. "We work-people of the Shears
and Iron." While he was at it, he annihilated all Zlodeyevka's leading citizens and rich men, and swore, as sure
as his name was Shimen-Eli, that they all ought to be
sent to Siberia.

"I tell you this, Reb Dudi!" he wound up his tirade.
"It is written: 'Dig not a pit for another....' The devil
take them all, those philanthropists of ours, I mean! All
they know is to suck the blood of us poor people and
fleece us alive! For a loan of three rubles I pay a quarter
a week—do you hear that! All right! I say nothing. But
they'll fall into other hands yet! Their time will come!
Don't you worry—they hold no guaranty from God yet!
My wife, that is, Tsipe-Beile-Reize—God bless her!—
says that I'm a good-for-nothing *shlimazl*, because if I
only wanted to I could put the fear of God into them. But
who listens to a wife? I have some say in the matter too.
Doesn't the Holy *Torah* say in black and white, 'And he
shall rule over thee...'? And do you know what that
means? Why, it's remarkable! Just listen! 'He'—that is,

the husband, 'shall rule over thee'—that's to say, over the wife! But you see what happens! 'He that falleth once shall fall again and again.' Once you have started pouring, pour me out another little glass. As it says in the Talmud: 'Askakoordi, debarbanti. . . .' "

Shimen-Eli's speech grew thicker as time went on. His eyes began to close, and soon he was leaning up against the wall, dozing. His head drooped sideways, his hands were folded on his chest, and he clutched the tip of his little goatee with three fingers like a man deep in thought. But for the fact that he shored and wheezed and made whistling noises with his nose, you would never have said that he was asleep. But though he dozed, his brain went on working, and he dreamt that he was at home, sitting at his work-table. On the table lay a queer garment, the nature of which you could not even guess at. To say that it was a pair of trousers—then where was the crotch? There wasn't a sign of any crotch! A waistcoat? Where did those long sleeves come from, then? And if it wasn't the one nor the other, then what was it? It couldn't be nothing! Shimen-Eli turns it inside out—and lo, it is a gaberdine! And what a gaberdine! Brand-new, shiny, satiny. He had not handled anything like it in all his born days! But what does he care! He takes a penknife out of his vest-pocket and begins to look for the seam to rip it open. It was a good thing that Tsipe-Beile-Reize happened to come in just then. She began to curse and swear at him:

"May you have your belly ripped open and your guts let out, you *shlimazl*, you, you green cucumber, you fine kidney bean, you! Can't you see that is your Sabbath gaberdine, which I had made for you out of the money we saved up from the goat!"

And Shimen-Eli remembered that, with God's help, he now had a goat. What a joy! He had never seen so many crocks of milk in all his life! So many bowls of cream cheese! And the butter—dishes full of butter! And the buttermilk, the whey, the clotted cream! And the piles and piles of rolls and butter buns sprinkled with powdered sugar and cinnamon! And the smell, the smell! A peculiar smell, a familiar one—ugh! Shimen-Eli felt something crawling up his neck, behind his ear and over his face. It tickled him, and the smell of it stunk in his nostrils. He passed his hand over his face and caught a bug. He opened one eye, then the other, and looked at the window. Goodness, woe is me! Day was already breaking!

"Well, I never! That was a pretty long doze!" Shimen-Eli said to himself with a twitch of his shoulders.

He woke up the innkeeper, ran out into the yard, opened the barn door, took the goat by the strap and hurried home like a man who is afraid that he will be late and miss God knows what.

Chapter Six

Tsipe-Beile-Reize, meanwhile, seeing that her husband was away so long, was wondering what it could mean. She had begun to think that maybe, God forbid, something had happened to him. What if robbers had fallen upon her husband on the way, taken all his money, then murdered him and thrown the body into a ditch? And now she, Tsipe-Beile-Reize, would be a widow for the rest of her days, all alone in the world with so many children on her hands—may the Evil Eye spare them! She might as well drown herself. She had not shut an eye all night for thinking thoughts like these. When the first cock crowed she jumped up and slipped on her dress, and went out on the doorstep to look out for her husband —please God he would come home safe. "What can you expect from such a *shlimazl*," she thought, working herself up to give him the warm welcome he deserved.

But when she saw Shimen-Eli leading the goat by his strap, she was so relieved that she greeted him quite affectionately.

"What a time you have been, my little birdie! I was beginning to think you had sunk into the earth, my precious, or some misfortune had happened to you, God forbid!"

Shimen-Eli untied the girdle, took the goat into the passage, and began pouring out his story like peas out of a sack so as not to give his wife time to think.

"Well, my wife, I have bought you a goat—do you hear? A goat of goats! The housewives here will have long to wait before they can ever dream of such a goat. And what does she eat? Almost nothing! Just a mash of bran once a day, with a little straw off the synagogue roof. As for milk—may the Evil Eye spare her—she's as good as a cow. She milks twice a day. I've seen a full milk-pail with my own eyes—may God let me see all of the best! A goat, did I say? She's a mother, not a goat! That's what she says—Teme-Gittel, I mean. It's a *metsiah*, I tell you—a bargain. She let me have it for six and a half rubles—dirt cheap! And the haggling I had to do! As a matter of fact she didn't want to sell at all. The job I had to persuade her! Chopping wood is easier! All night at it!"

And Tsipe-Beile-Reize, meanwhile, was thinking: "As for Nechame-Broche, may she have all the boils I wish her, with more to come! Thinks she's the only housewife in town, the only one who has a goat! I'd like to see how her eyes will pop out when she sees that Tsipe-Beile-Reize, the wife of Shimen-Eli, has a goat too! And Bluma-Zlata? And Chaya-Meite? Friends, they call themselves! May they have only half of what they wish me, God in heaven!"

Reflecting thus, she lit the stove and began to prepare noodles for a milk soup for breakfast, while Shimen-

Eli put on his *tallis* and *tfil.in* and began to say his prayers. He had not prayed for a long time with such earnestness and feeling as he did that day. Imitating the cantor, he sang the hosannas so loudly and with such a snapping of the fingers that he woke the children up. Learning from their mother that their father had brought home a goat and that she was cooking noodles with milk for breakfast, the children leapt out of bed in their undershirts, took hands and started to dance for sheer joy, the while they sang a song which they had just made up:

> *A goat, a goat!*
> *Papa has bought a goat!*
> *The goat will give milk,*
> *And Mamma will cook noodles!*

The sight of his singing and dancing children did Shimen-Eli's heart good. "Poor things," he thought, "they never have any milk. Never mind, though, they'll have plenty of it now, God help. Every day you'll get a glass of milk, *kasha* with milk, milk with your tea. A goat means everything. Who cares now for Fishel the butcher *baltakse*? I spit on him! He doesn't want to give meat? Gives only bones? Let him choke with them! What do I want his meat for when we have milk? For the Sabbath? For the Sabbath we can buy fish. Where does it stand written that you must only eat meat? I have come across no such law yet. If all the Jews only listened to me they would buy themselves goats. I'd like to see how that fat-bellied taxman of ours would look then! The devil take his father's father's father!

With these thoughts in his mind, Shimen-Eli *Shma-Ko-leinu* put away his prayer accessories, then washed his hands, cut the bread, and waited for the noodles and milk to be served. But at that moment the door flew open and in rushed Tsipe-Beile-Reize with an empty pail in her hands, her face livid. And upon the head of Shimen-Eli was loosed a torrent of curses and abuse. Nay, they were not curses—but stones raining from the heavens, fire and brimstone pouring out of Tsipe-Beile-Reize's mouth.

"May your father, the drunkard, be spewed out of his grave, and may you take his place! May you turn to stone, to a bone! May you sink into the earth! May you be shot with a gun, hanged and drowned, burned and roasted, cut up into little pieces! Go and have a look—you monster, you robber, you murderer—have a look at the goat you've brought me! A plague on your head, on your arms and legs—God in heaven, loving Father!"

The rest of it Shimen-Eli did not hear. Pulling his cap down, he went out of the house to see for himself the misfortune that had befallen him.

Coming outside and seeing the treasure he had bought standing tethered to a peg and calmly chewing the cud, he was utterly dumbfounded and did not know what to do, where to turn. He stood there for a while, thinking, then said to himself:

" 'Let my soul die with the Philistines!' But the devil will yet take that *melamed* and his wife! You can't play tricks with me! I'll show them tricks that'll make their eyes grow dark! He looked such an innocent, too, that *melamed*, above all worldly affairs. And now look! No wonder the boys giggled when he bundled me out with that goat! And his wife, too—wishing all that milk on me! I'll show them milk! I'll milk all the blood out of those Kozodoyevkites, the pious hypocrites, the swindlers, the scoffers!"

Saying which, Shimen-Eli *Shma-Koleinu* set out for Kozodoyevka once more with the intention of giving a "concert" (meaning "hell") to the *melamed* and his wife.

Seeing the innkeeper of Oak Inn standing in his doorway with his pipe in his teeth, our tailor burst out laughing while still at a distance.

"What's the fun?" asked Dudi. "What are you laughing at?"

"Please take a look, will you, maybe you'll laugh too," said the tailor, going into fits of laughter as though devils were tickling his ribs. "What do you think of such luck, Reb Dudi? 'All men are false-hearted'—there isn't a trouble that passes me by! It's a shame, I tell you! Did I get it hot from my wife, that is, Tsipe-Beile-Reize, God bless her! If I had half as many rubles as the number of curses she heaped on my head I would be a rich man. And I had to take it on an empty stomach too! May it all come true on that accursed *melamed* and his wife! Imagine me letting them get away with it, if you can! I shall give 'an eye for an eye'—tit for tat! If there is anything I hate it is to have tricks played on me! Come, Reb Dudi, give a man something to wet his throat with so that he has strength to speak—'thy rod and thy staff they comfort me.' Your health, Reb Dudi. As the Good Book says: 'Today the world trembles'—so cheer up! Don't you worry, I'll give them an earful! I'll show them how to play tricks on us work-people of the Shears and Iron, damn it!"

"Who told you it was a trick?" the innkeeper asked with feigned innocence, puffing away at his pipe. "Maybe you did not quite understand each other?"

Shimen-Eli jumped up at that.

"What a thing to say! What are you talking about? I go specially to buy a goat, and tell them in plain Yiddish, I want a goat, d'you understand—a g-o-a-t! And you tell me!"

Dudi went on smoking, shrugged his shoulders and spread his hands, as much as to say: "It's none of my doing, is it? It isn't my fault at all."

And Shimen-Eli took his goat off to Kozodoyevka, his anger burning high within him.

Chapter Seven

The *melamed*, meanwhile, was engaged in his business, that is, he was beating into his pupils' heads the same passage of the treatise concerning damages, and together they filled the synagogue yard with their loud chant: "And she, the cow, did strike the pitcher with her tail and did break it. . . ."

"Peace unto you, peace unto teachers and learners! Good-morning, Rabbi, to you and your pupils!" Shimen-Eli said, coming in. "Spare me a minute, pray. Nothing will happen: the cow will not run away, the pitcher will not mend itself. I will be brief: you have played a fine trick on me! Maybe it was a joke, but I don't mind telling you that I don't like such jokes. I daresay you have heard that story about the two men who were steaming themselves on the top shelf in the bath on Sabbath eve? One says to the other: 'Here's my birch switch, give me a warm-up.' And the other, without a word, took the birch switch, and gave him such a drubbing with it that he was all black and blue. Then the beaten one says: 'Look here, my friend. If you wanted to get even with me and took this opportunity while I was lying naked on the upper shelf and you had the switch in your hand, that's all very well. But if you meant it as a joke, then I don't mind telling you that I don't care for such jokes!' "

"What are you driving at?" asked the *melamed*, taking off his glasses and scratching his ear with them.

"I am driving at you and that fine goat of yours, which you palmed off on me by accident, just for the sake of the laugh. But you can laugh on the wrong side of your face sometimes, you know! Don't think you're dealing with just a nobody—a snotty-nose! I am Shimen-Eli of Zlodeyevka, one of the Shears and Iron and the *gabai* of the tailors' synagogue, damn it!"

Shimen-Eli uttered the last words with a skip—he was so worked up—and the *melamed* put on his glasses again and looked at him as one does at a raving patient. His pupils were choking with suppressed laughter.

" 'Sufficient unto the day is the evil thereof.' Why do you stare at me like an angry official?" Shimen-Eli demanded, now thoroughly exasperated. "I come here to buy a goat, and you palm off on me the devil knows what!"

"You don't like the goat?" the *melamed* asked amicably.

"A goat, did you say? If that's a goat, then you're the *gubernator!*"

The boys went into fits of laughter. Just then Teme-Gittel the Silent came in, and the real doings started. Shimen-Eli spoke, Teme-Gittel yelled, Chaim-Chone the Wise sat and looked, and the boys rocked with laughter. At last, Teme-Gittel lost her temper in real earnest, and seizing the tailor's arm, she dragged him out, saying:

"Come on! Let's go to the rabbi. Let people see how a Zlodeyevka tailor tries to pick faults at nothing! Making up all kinds of things! Slandering people!"

"Come on," said Shimen-Eli. "By all means, let people see how respectable folks, pious Jews, you might say, catch a strange man and try to make a fool of him. As it says in the prayer-book, 'We have become a mockery....' You come along, too, *melamed.*"

Chaim-Chone put a plush cap on over his skull-cap, and it was decided that all four were to go to the rabbi— the tailor, the *melamed*, the *melamed's* wife and the goat.

The delegation found the Chief Rabbi wiping his hands and saying his prayers after having relieved nature. He read the prayer slowly, rolling each word over on his tongue with relish. His devotions over, the rabbi drew his coat about him and seated himself in an armchair that had no bottom to it, being little more than feet and armrests, and was as shaky as an old man's teeth which should have fallen out long ago but still hold on by nothing short of a miracle.

After hearing out both sides, who had kept interrupting one another, the rabbi sent for the *dayan,* the *shochet* and other leading citizens of the town, and when these arrived, addressed the tailor in the following words: "Please tell the whole story again from beginning to end, and then she shall tell hers."

And the tailor Shimen-Eli readily repeated his story all over again. His name was Shimen-Eli, a tailor from the town of Zlodeyevka, one of the Shears and Iron work-people and *gabai* of the synagogue, although he had told them time and again, "I am unworthy of thy favours! 'I want neither thy honey nor thy sting.' Keep your honours and the kicks that go with them." And they say, "Kicks you will get but *gabai* you shall remain!" To make a long story short, he went to Kozodoyevka to buy himself a goat—the devil he needed it! But his wife, Tsipe-Beile-Reize—God bless her!—gave him no peace. She screamed, "I want a goat!" And since a wife, as you know, has to be obeyed, he came to *Melamed* Chaim-Chone to buy a goat, and bargained for one on the clear understanding that it was a goat. And what was the result? They took his money, and instead of a goat, they palmed off on him the devil knows what—probably as a joke. But he, Shimen-Eli, was not one to stand for such jokes. No doubt you have heard that story about the two men who were steaming themselves in the bath on *Shabbas* eve?

And Shimen-Eli repeated the bath story, and the rabbi and the other leading citizens nodded and smiled.

"Well," said the rabbi, "we have heard one side. Now let us hear the other."

Thereupon Chaim-Chone the Wise stood up, pulled his cap down over his skull-cap, and began in this wise:

"Hear me, dear sirs. Well, it was like this. There I was, sitting with my pupils, sitting and studying. Studying the Talmudic treatise on compensation for damages. Yes, well then ... in comes this man from Zlodeyevka, and says he is a Zlodeyevka inhabitant, that is, he comes from Zlodeyevka, if you know what I mean. Well then, he greets me, and tells me a whole story about his being from Zlodeyevka and having a wife named Tsipe-Beile-Reize.... It *is* Tsipe-Beile-Reize, isn't it?"

The *melamed* leaned over towards the tailor, who, fingering his little beard all the time, had been listening with his eyes shut and his head cocked on one side.

"You speak the truth," he answered. "She has all three names: Tsipe, and Beile, and Reize. She has been called that as long as I know her, which is upwards of thirty years, on and off. But let us hear what else you have to say, my dear friend. Don't beat about the bush! Stick to the point. Tell them what I said and what you said. In the words of Solomon the Wise: 'There is nothing new under the sun'—dodging won't help you."

"But I know nothing at all about it!" the *melamed* answered, frightened. Pointing to his wife, he went on: "She did all the talking, she made the deal with him. I had nothing at all to do with it."

"Then let us hear what she has to say," quoth the Rabbi, pointing to Teme-Gittel the Silent. She wiped her lips, propped her cheek up in one hand, and waving the other about in the air, poured forth her story in a rapid stream of words, without pausing for breath, her face aflame.

"Listen, this is how it was. This man here, this Zlodeyevka tailor—may he forgive me for saying it—is either mad or drunk or I don't know what! Who ever heard of such a thing? A man comes to me all the way from Zlodeyevka, and starts worrying the life out of me—sell him a goat (I had two of them). And he tells me a long rigmarole about not wanting to buy a goat at all because he had no need of it, only he had a wife, that is, Tsipe-Beile-Reize, who was set on having a goat, and wanted him to buy one for her, and a wife, he says, must be obeyed. You follow me? What's that got to do with me, I says? You want to buy a goat? All right, I'll sell you one, although, on the other hand, I wouldn't sell it for any money. What is money? Money rolls, money goes, but a goat remains a goat. And what a goat! A goat, did I say? She's a mother, not a goat! You ought to see how she milks—may the Evil Eye spare her! And how much milk she gives! And she doesn't eat hardly anything. A mash of bran once a day, for the rest a little straw off the roof of the synagogue. But then, you know, I thought: after all, I have two goats—may the Evil Eye spare them—and money is tempting. To make a long story short, my husband—God bless him—put in a word and we struck a bargain with the tailor. And how much do you think I got? May my enemies have as much as I got for that goat. So I gave him away the goat—may all my near and dear ones have such a goat! A goat, did I say? A mother, not a goat! And after that he comes and tries to blacken my name. That goat, he says, isn't a goat! I tell you what! Here she stands. Give me a milk-pail, somebody, and I'll milk her here right in front of you."

And she took a pail from the *rebbitzin*, milked the goat right there in front of everybody, then held it up for everyone to look in, beginning, naturally, with the rabbi, then the *dayan*, then the other leading men of the town, and only after that all the rest of the company.

The uproar in the rabbi's house was dreadful. One shouted, "We ought to make this Zlodeyevka tailor pay for it! Let him stand us all drinks!" Another said, "That isn't enough. He ought to have his goat taken away from him!" A third said, "No, leave the goat alone. Let him keep her and grow old with her in riches and honour.

What we ought to do is give him a few good cuffs and kick him out to the devil together with his goat!"

Seeing the turn events were taking, Shimen-Eli slipped out of the rabbi's house on the quiet and betook himself off.

Chapter Eight

And so Shimen-Eli took his feet on his shoulders, as the saying goes, and sped home with his goat like a man running away from a fire. He looked back to see if anyone was after him, and thanked God for having got away "gratis," that is, without a single cuff.

As he approached Oak Inn, he said to himself, "I'll be hanged if I tell him anything!" And he kept it all back from Dudi.

"Well, what's the news?" the latter asked with feigned interest.

"What news can there be?" answered Shimen-Eli. "People are afraid of me, you know. I'm not one to stand any nonsense. 'Thou art a man'—I'm not a schoolboy! I opened my mouth upon them and had a learned argument with the *melamed,* in which I simply wiped the floor with him. To make a long story short, he begged my pardon and gave me back the goat I had bought from them. Here she is. 'Take thou the soul, and the fortune give to me'— take this animal away, and give me a glass of vodka."

"He is not only a braggart, but a liar into the bargain!" thought the innkeeper. "I'll have to play the same trick on him again. We'll hear what he will say then."

To the tailor he said:

"I have just the thing for you, Shimen-Eli—a glass of old cherry wine, if you feel like it."

"A delicacy from heaven!" said Shimen-Eli, and licked his lips. "Well, well, let's try it, I'll tell you what I think of it. I doubt not that you keep good cherry wine, but 'not all men are false,' that is, not everybody understands a good thing."

The tailor's tongue loosened after the very first glass.

"Tell me this, my dear kinsman," he said. "You are no fool and have dealings with many people. Tell me, do you believe in witchcraft, in sorcery?"

"Meaning?" asked Dudi, pretending to be puzzled.

"Exactly. In *dybbuks*, in devils, in evil spirits, in ghosts!"

"Why do you ask?" Dudi said in the same innocent manner, puffing at his pipe.

"Just like that," answered Shimen-Eli, and went on talking about wandering souls, about witches and sorcerers, about ghosts, ghouls, and vampires. Dudi pretended to be listening attentively, puffing at his pipe, then he spat and said:

"Do you know what, Shimen-Eli? I'll be afraid to sleep tonight, if you ask me. To tell you the truth, I have always been afraid of dead people, but now I'm beginning to believe in ghosts and jesters and all the rest of it."

"What can you do?" answered the tailor. "Try not to believe! Just let some unclean spirit get into your house, and it will be up to all kinds of tricks—upset the pot with your *borshch*, empty the water barrel and all your pitchers, smash up all your crockery, and throw a cat into your bed so that it lies on your chest like a ton weight and you can't move. And when you wake up, you find the cat staring straight into your face like a sinful human being. ..."

"Sha! Enough!" cried the innkeeper, spitting to ward off evil spirits and waving his arms. "Don't tell me such horrors before bedtime!"

"Well, good-bye, Reb Dudi, forgive me if I have been a nuisance. It's not my fault, you know. How is it written? —'There were not words enough'—the old woman didn't have troubles enough, so she went and bought a pig. ... Good-night."

Chapter Nine

Upon returning to Zlodeyevka, the tailor entered his house with a frown upon his face, determined to tell his wife off properly the way she deserved. However, he controlled himself and kept his temper. "A woman remains a woman," he thought. "What can you expect from her? Let it go!" And for the sake of peace and quiet he told her this story, which he had made up on the spur of the moment.

"What shall I tell you, Tsipe-Beile-Reize! If you ask me, people are really afraid of me a bit. As to how I told off the *melamed* and that wife of his, I leave you to imagine. I gave it to them hot! More, I dragged them off to the rabbi, and the rabbi decided they should pay me a fine, because when a man like Shimen-Eli comes to them to buy a goat they ought to consider it a great honour, because Shimen-Eli, says the rabbi, is not the kind of man, who—"

But Tsipe-Beile-Reize had no desire to hear her husband's praises. She was eager to see the real goat he had now come home with. So snatching a pail, she ran out. By and by Tsipe-Beile-Reize came running in again. This time she said nothing, but seized her husband by the scruff of his neck, fetched him three hard knocks, and pushed him out "to all the devils and the devil's teeth" together with his belauded goat.

Outside, a crowd gathered round the tailor and the goat. Men, women and children flocked together to hear the strange things that Shimen-Eli had to tell. Now this goat, which he was holding by her tether, was really a goat only in Kozodoyevka: there she gave milk, and could be milked. But the moment he came here with her she ceased to be a she-goat. Shimen-Eli swore with many oaths—you would have believed even a *meshumad* who swore like that—that he had seen the goat milked with his own eyes in the rabbi's house—a full pail of milk!

More people kept coming up; they stopped, examined the goat with interest, made the tailor repeat the story over and over again, and wondered greatly at it. Some laughed and cracked jokes, others shook their heads, spat, and said: "A fine goat that is! If she's a goat then I'm a *rebbitzin*!"

"Then what is it?"

"A *dybbuk*! Can't you see it's a *dybbuk*?"

The word "*dybbuk*" was caught up by the crowd. Hair-raising stories about *dybbuks* went round—stories of things that had happened right there in Zlodeyevka and in Kozodoyevka, and in Yampol, and in Pishi-Yabeda, and in Khaplapovich, and in Pechi-Khvost—and all over the world. Who had not heard the story of Leizer-Wolff's nag, which had had to be taken outside the town, killed and buried in a shroud? Or about the quarter of a fowl, which, on being served for the Sabbath meal, had started to flap its wing? There are any amount of such true stories!

When Shimen-Eli proceeded on his way, a band of urchins escorted him with great pomp, shouting after him:

"Hurray! Three cheers for the milking tailor!"

And the crowd held their sides with laughter.

This touched Shimen-Eli on the raw. Not enough that he had had this misfortune happen to him, they were making a laughing-stock of him too. So he went through the town with his goat and lifted his voice in loud complaint to the brethren of the Shears and Iron. How could you be silent at such an outrage! He told them all about what he had had done to him in Kozodoyevka, and showed them the goat. The brotherhood sent at once for vodka, and decided to go to the rabbi, the *dayans*, and the other leading citizens with clamorous protest: "Who ever heard of such a thing! It's an evil deed! To cheat a poor tailor out of his last few rubles and sell him the devil knows what for a goat! And making mock of him on top of it a second time! Not even in Sodom had anything like it been known!"

The rabbi and the *dayans* and other leading citizens heard out this complaint, and that same evening they held a meeting at the rabbi's where it was decided that an impressive letter should there and then be written to the rabbi, the *dayans* and other leading citizens of Kozodoyevka. And so the Zlodeyevka rabbi, *dayans* and other leading citizens composed a letter to the Kozodoyevka rabbis, *dayans* and other leading citizens in lofty and eloquent Hebrew. Here is the letter, word for word:

"To the Rabbis, *Dayans*, Sages, Illustrious scholars, the Pillars who uphold the entire House of Israel. Peace be upon you, peace be upon all the Jews of the sacred community of Kozodoyevka, may all good fortune come unto them. Amen!

"Whereas it has come to our ears that a great wrong has been done one of our townsmen—Reb Shimen-Eli, the son of Bendit-Leib, the tailor, known as Shimen-Eli *Shma-Koleinu*, namely: two of your citizens—*Melamed* Reb Chaim-Chone and his wife Teme-Gittel—may the Name bless her—did trick our tailor out of the sum of six rubles fifty kopeks in silver, which they did convert to their own use, wiping their lips and saying, 'We have done no wrong.' Such things are not done among Jews! We all, the undersigned, hereby testify that the said tailor is a poor hardworking man with a family, which he supports by honest labour. As King David has long since said in the Book of Psalms: 'When thou eatest the labour of thy hands, happy shalt thou be, and it shall be well with thee,' which dictum our wise men interpret to mean— 'Blessed wilt thou be in this world and the next.' Therefore do we beg you to make immediate and thorough inquiries respecting this matter we speak of, and may your judgement rise up like the sun! You must adjudge one of the two: either our tailor must have his money refunded to him in full, or he must be given back the goat that he bought, for the one which he brought home with him is not a goat at all! Our whole town is prepared to swear to that. So let there be peace among the Jews, according to the word of our sages: There is no more perfect vessel of grace to the Jews than peace. Therefore peace be with you, peace to those near and to those far, peace unto all the Jews. Amen!

"From us, your slaves, whose thighs are thinner than your little fingers:

"Rabbi, son of a rabbi—may he enjoy the blessings of Paradise....

"And rabbi, son of a rabbi—may he enjoy the blessings of Paradise....

"And Boruch Kapota, Zorach Pupik, Fishel Vikidailo, Chaim Kvitch, Nisel Katchan, Motel Sholechts, Shie-Heshel Kishkish."

Chapter Ten

That night the moon shone brightly and looked down upon Zlodeyevka with its squalid huddle of tumbledown little houses without yards, without trees, without fences. The town at night looked like a cemetery with crumbling gravestones, some of which seemed to have dropped on their knees, and would long ago have tumbled down had they not been propped up by logs. And although the air here was none too fresh, and the odours wafted up from the market-place and the synagogue yard could hardly be called delightful, and the dust hung about as thick as a wall—nevertheless the people had crawled out into the open like cockroaches from their chinks—men and women, old people and children—to "take the fresh air" after the stifling heat of day. They sat about on their doorsteps, chatting, gossiping, or just gazing at the sky, looking at the face of the moon and the myriads of stars that, had you eighteen heads on your shoulders, you could never count.

That night Shimen-Eli the tailor, alone with the *metsiah* which he had bought in Kozodoyevka, wandered about the back streets of his little town, trying to keep out of the way of the urchins. He intended to set out on his journey at daybreak, and meantime he had dropped in at Hodel's tavern to cheer his drooping soul with a glass of vodka, unburden his heart and seek sympathy and advice in his sad plight.

Hodel the tavern-keeper was a widow with "a man's head on her shoulders," who hobnobbed with the government officials and was a good sister to all the workingmen in the town. She was known as the "excise-girl." She came by this nickname in the following way. As a girl she had been extremely good-looking—a real beauty, in fact. One day the exciseman, a very rich official, saw her as he was passing through Zlodeyevka. Hodel was taking some geese to the *shochet* to be slaughtered. The excise officer stopped her and asked, "Whose are you, little girl?"

She laughed shyly and ran away. Ever since then she had been known as the "excise-girl." Some, though, say that the officer went to her home afterwards and spoke to her father Nechemye the Distiller. He wanted to marry her, and was willing to take her without a dowry, and to even pay the father. They were as good as getting betrothed, but tongues began to wag in the town and the match fell through. Hodel was afterwards married to some wretch of an epileptic. She cried bitterly, did not want to marry him. The whole town was on its head with excitement! People said she was crazy over the exciseman, and even made up a song about her, which the women and girls of Zlodeyevka sing to this day. It starts like this:

> *The moon shone,*
> *It was late at night,*
> *And Hodele sat at her door...*

And it ended with these words:

> *I love you, my darling,*
> *I love you without end,*
> *And I cannot live without you!*

Well then, it was to this "excise-girl" Hodel that our tailor came to pour his heart out, to tell her his sad story, and ask her advice—what to do?

"What to do? For you are indeed as wise as you are beautiful—'black and comely,' as King David says in *The Song of Songs*. Tell me what to do."

"What to do?" said Hodel, and spat out. "Can't you see it's a *dybbuk*? Much good it will do you! Why don't you get rid of the thing? The same may happen to you as happened to my Aunt Pearl—God save us, may she rest in peace."

"And what was that?" Shimen-Eli asked in alarm.

"This," answered Hodel with a sigh. "My Aunt Pearl—may she enjoy the blessings of Paradise—was a pious, God-fearing woman. It runs in the family.... Though here, in this accursed Zlodeyevka, may it burn to the ground, everyone likes to run down everyone else—behind his back, of course. But to your eyes they'll flatter you and fawn on you—dearie this, darling that. Well, then, my Aunt Pearl—may she rest in peace—went to the market one day, and on the ground in front of her what should she see but a ball of thread. 'A ball of thread,' she thought, 'may come in handy.' So she bent down and picked it up. Picked up the ball of thread and went on further, when it up and jumped in her face and fell to the ground. Auntie, of course, bends down and picks it up again, and gain it up and jumps in her face and then falls to the ground. Auntie bent down a third time and picks up the ball—and again the same thing happens. So she gave it up in disgust—the devil take it—and made to go home. And would you believe it—there was the ball of thread rolling after her! She started to run, but the ball went after her faster! To make a long story short, she came home more dead than alive, dropped down in a faint, and was poorly for nearly a whole year afterwards. Now what do you think that was? Guess!"

"Pooh! All women are cut out on the same pattern!" said the tailor. "Old wives' tales, nonsense, foolishness! If you listened to everything women chattered about you'd be afraid of your own shadow. Verily it is written: 'Woman, thou art fickle'—women are just silly geese. But never mind. 'Today the world trembles'—so cheer up. Good-night to you."

And Shimen-Eli went on his way.

It was a starry night. The moon rode the skies between tattered clouds that looked like dark mountains trimmed with silver. The moon glanced askance at Zlodeyevka, which was sunk deep in slumber. Many of the inhabitants, to escape the bugs, had moved their beds out into the open, and slept with yellow sheets pulled up over their heads, snoring lustily and dreaming sweet dreams of market earnings, brisk trade, and large profits; others dreamt of kind landlords, profitable deals, a regular livelihood, honourable work, or just the honour alone—all kinds of dreams.

There was not a soul astir, not a murmur. Even the market dogs, who had barked themselves hoarse and run themselves off their legs the whole day, crawled in between the horse troughs, hid their muzzles in their paws, and slept. Only once in a while one of them would growl in his sleep when he dreamt of a bone that other dogs were coveting, or when a fly got into his ear and became confidential. Now and then a silly beetle would fly past on spread wings, start spinning round on one spot, buzzing like the string of a double-bass—zh-zh-zh-zh—then drop to the ground with a smack and be silent. Even the night watchman who went about the town keeping an eye on the shops and shaking his rattle—kla-kla-kla—even he, on that night of all nights, had had a drink, and sat fast asleep propped up against a wall.

And on that still night Shimen-Eli the tailor roams about the town all by himself, not knowing whether to move on, to stand still or to sit down. He goes along, muttering to himself:

" 'Came the cat and devoured the goat. . . .'* The old woman did not have troubles enough, so she went and bought a horse. . . . Curse that goat! Nanny-goat, little kid, goatie! Ha, ha, ha!"

And he bursts out laughing, and jumps at the sound of his own voice. Just at that moment he passes by the "cold *shool*," where, it is said, dead men in white shrouds and praying-shawls pray every Saturday night. And it seems to the tailor that he hears weird singing—whoo-whoo!—like the wind howling in the chimney on a winter night. He hurries away from the "cold *shool*" and wanders down the "Russian" street. And all of a sudden he hears the shrill hoot of an owl, which stands on the very top of the Church dome. Sheer terror grips the tailor. But he pulls himself together and tries to recollect the words of the verse that is uttered at night to drive fear away, but the verse has faded out of his mind. And as if on purpose there floats before his eyes the gruesome images of friends and acquaintances long since dead. There leaps to his mind all the stories he had ever heard in the course of his life about devils, and *dybbuks*, and ghouls in the

* From an allegorical ballad in the *Seder* home service.—*Tr*

guise of calves, and goblins that rush about as if on wheels, and vampires who walk on their hands, and one-eyed monsters. He recalls the stories about the dead who come to life and wander about the world in their shrouds together with the souls of sinners. Shimen-Eli had quite made up his mind that the goat he was dragging about with him was not a goat at all, but a werewolf or something, an evil spirit. He would not be surprised to see it stick out a long flickering tongue, or flap a pair of wings, and wake the whole town with a loud cock-a-doodle-doo! Shimen-Eli felt his hair standing up on end. He stopped, and undid the strap, hoping thus to be rid of his companion. But no such luck! The goat didn't think of leaving him. It would not budge an inch. Shimen-Eli tried moving forward: the goat moved forward too. He turned to the right—so did the goat. He turned to the left, and the goat turned left.

"*Shma Yisroel!*" screamed the tailor, and ran off as fast as his legs could carry him. And as he ran he thought he could hear someone chasing him and bleating in a thin goat-like voice, like a human being, or singing like a cantor in the synagogue, "God will make the dead alive in the abundance of his kindness."

Chapter Eleven

In the morning, when the men got up to go to the synagogue, the women to the market, and the girls to drive the cows out into the herd, they found the tailor sitting on the ground. Next to him, chewing the cud and wagging its beard, sat the goat of ill fame. People went up to Shimen-Eli and tried to speak to him, but he did not answer. He sat there like a graven image with staring eyes. A crowd collected, people came running up from all over the town. There was a hubbub and uproar, everyone jabbering excitedly. Conjecture ran wild: Shimen-

Eli ... goat ... *Shma-Koleinu* ... *dybbuk* ... fiends ... vampires ... the Evil One ... riding on his back all night ... the poor man half-killed ... killed. ... And each vied with the other in making up stories of how they had seen It riding on his back.

"Who rode on whose back?" one man asked, poking his head through the dense circle. "Shimen-Eli on the goat's, or the goat on Shimen-Eli's?"

The crowd burst out laughing.

"Woe to you and woe to your laughter!" said one of the craftsmen. "Bearded men! Married men! Fathers of families! Shame on you! Standing around guffawing? Can't you see that the tailor is not himself, he is a dying man? Instead of standing there grinning and jabbering— the devil take your father's father's father!—it would be better if you took him home and sent for the doctor!"

The man shot these words out like a gun, and the crowd was at once silenced. One ran to fetch some water, another ran off to call Yudel, the healer. They took Shimen-Eli under the arms, led him home and put him to bed. By and by the healer Yudel came with all his stock in trade and fell to work saving the tailor. He applied cupping-glasses and leeches, tapped a vein and drew blood.

"The more blood we draw," said Yudel, "the better he will be, because all illnesses—touch wood!—come from inside, they are in the blood."

Having thus explained the mysteries of the medical art, Yudel the healer left, promising to call again in the evening.

And Tsipe-Beile-Reize, looking at her husband who lay stretched out, poor fellow, on the rickety trestle-bed, covered with rags, his eyes rolled up, his lips parched— raving with fever, she began to wring her hands and beat her head against the wall, wailing and weeping as one does for the dead.

"Woe is me, may I be struck dead by lightning! Who are you leaving me for with little children on my hands?"

And the little children, naked and barefoot, huddled round the woebegone mother in a weeping chorus. The elder ones wept quietly, hiding their faces and swallowing their tears; the younger ones, not understanding what it was all about, sobbed out loud and ever louder. And the youngest of the lot, a boy of three with a yellow emaciated face and a big belly, tottered up to his mother on his crooked little legs, threw his little arms round her neck and cried: "Mama, I am hungry!"

The sight and sound of that wailing chorus was more than people could bear. Everyone who came in to see the tailor hurried out broken-hearted, and when asked: "How is Shimen-Eli?", merely waved his hand with a hopeless gesture, as though to say, "Poor Shimen-Eli, what is there to say?"

Some next-door neighbours stood round with tearful faces and reddened noses, gazing sorrowfully at Tsipe-Beile-Reize, while their mouths worked painfully, and they shook their heads as much as to say, "Woe, woe to thee, poor Tsipe-Beile-Reize!"

It's a remarkable thing! For fifty years had Shimen-Eli *Shma-Koleinu* lived in Zlodeyevka, lived in squalor and want, forgotten by the world, like a worm in the darkness, and no one had cared about him, no one had known what kind of man he was. And now that he was ill, perhaps dying, all his virtues and merits had suddenly come to light. Everyone suddenly began speaking about him: the very soul of kindness, so pure of heart, such a generous philanthropist, that is, he had wrung as much as he could from the rich and given it to the poor, had fought for those poor tooth and nail, and shared his last crust with his neighbours. This and a lot more was said about the poor tailor, said in the tone which people generally use when speaking of the dead at their funerals. Practically the whole town came to see him and do what they could to save him from dying, God forbid, before his time.

Chapter Twelve

Meanwhile the brethren of the Shears and Iron held a meeting at Hodel's, the excise-girl's, ordered vodka, shouted, bawled, fumed against the rich, and called them all the names they could think of—behind their backs, of course.

"A fine town, this Zlodeyevka, may it burn to the ground! Why don't they do something, these rich men of ours—may they sink into the earth! Anybody who wants can suck our blood, and there's no one to stand up for us! Who pays all the blessed taxes? We do! And what about those plagues—the *shochet*, say, the bath-house—God forgive us for mentioning them in the same breath—who are skinned alive to keep them? We are! Then why don't we do something? Let us go to our rabbis, and our *dayans*, and our leading citizens, and draw the guts out of them! It's a crying shame—a whole family done to death! Let us do something about it!"

And the brethren of the Shears and Iron betook themselves to the rabbi and kicked up a row. Whereupon the rabbi read out to them the reply which had just been received from the rabbis, the *dayans* and the leading citizens of Kozodoyevka through a *balagula*.

This is what the letter said:

"To the Rabbis, *Dayans*, and Illustrious Sages of the town of Zlodeyevka. Peace be upon you, and may your lights never be dimmed. Amen!

"Immediately upon receiving your epistle, which was sweeter than honey to our lips, we foregathered all and carefully went into the matter in question, upon which we came to the conclusion that members of our community have been wrongfully accused. On the face of it, this tailor of yours is a mean person who is guilty of slander and has created scandal between our two communities. He deserves to be severely punished. We, the undersigned, are prepared to bear witness under oath that we have seen the said goat milked with our own eyes—may all the goats of Israel milk no worse! Listen not to that tailor of yours, believe not his stories. Turn not your ears to unworthy speeches! May the mouths be stopped that utter lies. Peace unto you, peace unto all Jews from now and for all time!

"From your younger brethren prostrated in the dust at your feet:

"Signed: Rabbi so-and-so, the son of rabbi so-and-so— may his soul rest in peace, and rabbi so-and-so, the son of rabbi so-and-so—may his soul rest in peace.... Genech Gorgel, Kusiel Shmarovidlo, Shepsel Kartofel, Fishel Kachalka, Berel Vodka, Leib Vorechok, Eley Petelele."

When the rabbi had finished reading this letter, the Devout Toilers waxed more indignant than ever. "Aha! So those Kozodoyevka scoffers are trying to make fun of us! We'll show them who they are dealing with! Shears and Iron!"

Another meeting was held there and then, more vodka was sent for, and it was decided to take the blessed goat, go straight off to Kozodoyevka, and turn the whole place upside down there together with the *melamed* and his *cheder*.

So said, so done. They mustered about sixty strong— tailors, bootmakers, carpenters, blacksmiths and butchers, stalwarts all, picked men, armed each with his tools: this one with a yardstick, that one with a press iron, one with a last, another with a meat axe, a third with a ham-

mer, while some took with them various household uten-
sils—a rolling-pin, a grater, a chopper. It was decided
to make war on Kozodoyevka—to sack the town, kill,
ravage!

"Once for all!" shouted the warriors. " 'Let us die with
the Philistines!' Let us wipe them out and be done with
it!"

"Wait a minute there," one of the Devout Toilers suddenly called out. "You are ready to go forth? You have
girded up your loins? But what about 'the lamb'? Where
is the goat?"

"That's right, where has that *dybbuk* gone to?"

"He's disappeared!"

"He's not such a fool of a *dybbuk* after all! But where
could he have gone to?"

"Run home, I daresay. Back to his *melamed.* What a
question to ask!"

"Of all the crazy things! You reason like an ass!"

"From an ass I hear it! Where else could he go?"

"What's the use of arguing? You can scream from today till tomorrow—but 'the child is lost.' The goat has
disappeared!"

Chapter Thirteen

Let us now leave the bewitched tailor, battling with the
Angel of Death, and the town's Devout Toilers, girding
themselves for war, and pass on to the *dybbuk*, that is,
the goat.

Seeing what an uproar and tumult had arisen in the
town, our hero said to himself: "What do I want all this
bother and headache for? What's the good of being tied
up to a tailor and being dragged about all over the place
with that *shlimazl* till you die of starvation? Would it not
be better to just run away, no matter where? Anything
is better than such a life."

And so that wise animal made a bolt for it! He dashed off like mad across the market-place, jumping over men and women, causing people damage and playing havoc with everything. He upset tables with loaves and buns, and baskets with cherries and currants, he skipped over crockery and glassware, kicking, scattering and smashing everything that got in his way. The women, scared out of their wits, screamed: "Who is it? What is it? Gott in Himmel! A goat! A *dybbuk*! Woe is me! Where is he? There he is! Catch him! Catch him quick!"

And a whole crowd of men with coats tucked up, and women with—excuse me—skirts hitched up were soon in full cry. But it was no use. Our goat had tasted the sweet of freedom, and nothing on earth could stop him now!

"And the unhappy tailor? The moral of the piece?" the reader will ask.

Do not insist, children! The end was not a happy one, It all began very cheerfully, but ended, like most cheerful stories, very sadly.

And since you know that the author of this story is not a gloomy soul who prefers a melancholy tale to a funny one, and that there is nothing he hates more than pointing a moral, he begs to take leave of you with an amused chuckle, and the wish that Jews and all people the world over should have more cause to laugh than to cry.

Laughter is good for the health. The doctors advise us to laugh.

1900

IF I WERE ROTHSCHILD

I were Rothschild ..." the Kasrilovka *melamed*
let his imagination run away with him one Thursday
morning, after his wife had demanded money for the
Sabbath and he had had none to give her. Ah, if I were
Rothschild! Do you know what I would do? First of all
I would make it a rule that a wife should always have a
three-ruble note on her and not bother a man every time
Thursday comes round and there's nothing to provide for
the Sabbath. Secondly, I would take my Sabbath gaberdine out of the pawn.... No I wouldn't! I would buy out
the wife's catskin burnoose, so she should not nag me
any more about feeling cold. Then I'd buy the whole of
this house with all its three rooms, including the pantry,
and the lumber-room, and the cellar, and the loft, and
all that goes with it, so she shouldn't talk any more about
living cramped. Here are two rooms for you—cook, bake,
chop your cabbage, do your washing, do what you want,
only leave me in peace to work with my pupils on a fresh
head! No worrying about making a living, about getting
money to provide for the Sabbath—what a blessing! I
would marry off my daughters, and get that burden off

my shoulders. What more do I need? This is when I begin to turn my mind to community affairs.

First of all I would donate a new roof to the old synagogue, so's Jews should not have rain dripping on their heads when they are worshipping. The bath-house—may I be forgiven for mentioning them in the same breath—I would have completely rebuilt, because any day—God forbid!—you can expect an accident there, and who knows but that it might not happen on women's day of all days! And talking about the bath-house, then what should we say about the poor-house? It's about time it was pulled down and a hospital built in its place, you know—a real hospital with beds in it, and a doctor, and medicines, and chicken soup for the patients every day, the way they do it in all decent towns. Then I would build a home for the old, so's the old Talmud scholars should not have to sit around the stove in *Bes Hamedresh*. I'll set up a "Clothe the Naked" Society, so's the children of the poor should not run about—excuse me—with bare backsides, and a charitable Loan Society, so's a Jew, be he a *melamed* or a workman, or even a tradesman for that matter, should not have to pay interest and pawn the shirt off his back; I'll found a Board of Guardians for Marriageable Maidens so that girls over age from poor families could be decently clothed and helped to get married. I'd start lots of similar societies here in Kasrilovka. But why only in our Kasrilovka? I'll set up such societies wherever there are Jews living—everywhere, all over the world!

And for the sake of proper order, so's everything should be just so, do you know what I'll do? I'll set up one big charitable society to look after all the other societies, to take care of all the Jews, that is, all the people, so that people everywhere should be able to make a living, should live together in friendship, and sit in the *yeshivas*, and study the Bible and the Talmud with all its commentaries, its supplements and what not, and all the languages of the world. And over all the *yeshivas* I'd put one chief *yeshiva*—a Jewish academy—in Vilno, of course. From here would come the greatest scholars and sages in the world—and all for nothing, "at the expense of the rich," at my expense, that is, and things would be run strictly according to plan, so's there should be none of that "you me-I you-grab-nab" business, and everyone should have only one care—the common good. And what must we do to have people think of the common good? We must provide for every single person. Provide what? A living, of course. To make a living, as you know, is the main thing. Without a living there is no friendship. For the sake of a crust of bread people—God help them—are prepared to ruin each other, cut each other's throats, poison each other. Even our enemies, our ill-wishers all over the world—what do you think they want of us? Nothing. It's this business of making a living that's at the bottom of it all. If they were better off they wouldn't be half so nasty. Making money leads to envy, and envy to animosity, which is the cause of all woes and afflictions, persecutions, killings, brutalities, wars.

Ah, wars, wars! I tell you, they are a curse to the world! If I were Rothschild I would put an end to wars once and for all.

I suppose you will ask me—how? Very simple—with the help of money. Namely? Let me explain.

Two countries, say, are quarrelling over nothing, over a patch of land that isn't worth a pinch of snuff. "Territory"—they call it. One country says this and that territory belongs to her, while the other says, "No, it's mine!" Since the beginning of time God had created that patch of land specially for her. But up comes a third country and says, "You are both donkeys! This territory belongs to everyone, it is, so to speak, 'common property.'" To make a long story short, territory here, territory there—the end of it is that rifles and cannons start going off, men slaughter one another like sheep, and blood, blood flows like water.

But just imagine me coming to them at the very start and saying, "*Sha*, brothers, let me put a word in! What's the argument about? You think we don't understand what you are after? You don't care for the gibble-gabble, it's the *tsimmes* you want. Territory is just an excuse. The *gelt*—that's what you're after. And once it's a matter of *gelt*, then who's the man people come to for a loan? To me, to Rothschild, that is." And I say to them, "Do you know what? Here, you lanky Englishman in the checkered trousers, here's a billion for you! Here, you silly Turk in the red fez, here's a billion for you! And here, Auntie Reizel,* here's a billion for you! *Nu*? With God's help you'll pay me back with interest—not a big interest, God forbid—let's say four or five per cent. I'm a reasonable man, I don't want to get rich on you...."

Do you follow me? I've done a *gescheft*, and people stop slaughtering one another like cattle for no reason whatever. And once wars are done with, then who wants all these weapons and troops, the thunder of the captains and the shouting—the whole mishmash? They're useless. And once there are no weapons, no troops, no thunder and shouting—then that means there is no more envy, no more animosity, no more Turks, Englishmen, Frenchmen, Gypsies, or Jews—the whole world will then wear a different look. As it says in the scripture: "And there came the day...," that is, the day of the coming of the Messiah. (*A pause.*)

What? It's quite possible. If I were Rothschild maybe I would do away with money altogether. Let there be no money! Now I ask you—what is money? Don't let us deceive ourselves—money, if you want to know, is just a hoax, a delusion. People have taken a piece of paper,

* *Auntie Reizel*— Russia.—*Tr.*

printed a picture on it and written down on it: "Three rubles silver." Money, I tell you, is a sheer temptation, a lust, one of the most ruinous passions. Everyone is out to make it and no one has it. But if money just didn't exist at all in the world, there would be no work for the Tempter, and lust itself would cease to be! Do you follow what I mean?

But that's all very well. The question is—where would Jews get the money to provide for the Sabbath? (*Musingly.*) If it comes to that, where am I to get the money to keep this Sabbath?

1902

THE POT

must have your decision, Rabbi. It's a very important question. I don't know whether you know me—you may or you may not—I am Yenta, Yenta the chicken-peddler. I sell eggs, you know, eggs, and chickens, and geese, and ducks. I have my regular customers—you know, two or three houses—God bless them, they keep me going. If I had to pay interest, God forbid, I'd be up the spout long ago. As it is, I borrow a couple of rubles here, give it back there, borrow there, pay back here, and so we make a living somehow. Say what you like, but if my husband—God rest his soul— was alive today—te-te-te! I don't mind telling you, though, my life with him was not all honey either; between you and me he wasn't much of a bread-winner, he wasn't—may I be forgiven for saying so. He'd sit poring over his Talmud, sit there learning while I worked my fingers to the bone. True, I was used to working hard since I was a child, my mother brought me up that way—may her soul rest in peace; Bassy, her name was, Bassy the Candle-Maker; used to buy up fat from the butcher, you know, and make candles, thin candles, you know; those days they didn't have paraffin, and oil-lamps, and these glass chimneys that keep cracking—not a week goes by with me without one of them cracking.

What was I going to say? Oh, yes. You say, dying young.... When my Moishe-Benzion died—God rest his soul—he was twenty-six years old. You ask, how do I make it twenty-six? Well, he was nineteen at our wedding, and it's eight years since he died. Well then, nineteen and eight make twenty-three. Why not twenty-six? Because I didn't count the seven years he was ill. If you want to know, he was ill much longer than that; he always was poorly, I mean—he was always well, except for that cough of his—it killed him in the end, that cough did. He was always coughing, that is—not always, really, but only when the fit came on; he'd cough then something dreadful! The doctors said it was spasms or something; if you got them you might cough and you might not, it all depends. If you ask me it's all *shtram-gram*—nonsense! May goats know how to jump into neighbours' gardens as the doctors know what they are talking about. Take the son of Reb Aaron, the *shochet*. Yukel, his name is. Well, this Yukel had a toothache. And what they didn't do to him! They tried everything, but it was no use. So what does Yukel go and do? He puts garlic in his ear. They say garlic is wonderful for the toothache, but the pain got so bad that he nearly crawled up the walls with it, but he did not say a word about what he had done to himself. Along comes the doctor and feels his pulse. The fool, what has his pulse got to do with it? Good they took him to Yegupetz, otherwise he'd be—you know where? Where his sister is—she died in child-birth from the Evil Eye—God save you from it!

What was I going to say? Oh, yes. You say, a widow.... I became a widow very young, and was left with a baby on my hands and half a house in Poverty Street, next door to Leizer the carpenter, if you know

119

him—he lives not far from the baths. You ask—why only half a house? Because the other half isn't mine, it belongs to my brother-in-law, it does. Azriel, his name is. He's from Veselokut, you know, a small town; he deals in fish, he does, makes a mint of money, touch wood. It all depends on the weather, though; when the weather's good then the fish catch well, so the price comes down, but when it's windy then you don't catch any fish, so the price goes up; but it's better to catch fish and have the price come down. At least, that's what Azriel says. "But where's the sense?" I ask him. "The sense," he says, "is this: if the weather's good you catch fish, and if you catch fish the price comes down; but if it's windy, you don't catch fish, and if you don't catch fish the price goes up. So it's better to catch fish and have the price come down." "Yes," I says, "but where's the sense?" And he comes back again: "The sense," he says, "is this: if the weather's good, you catch fish, and if you catch fish the price comes down...." *Tfui*, bother the man! What's the good of talking to an ignoramus!

What was I going to say? Oh, yes. You say, to have your own home.... Naturally—it's better to have your own little corner than to knock about in strange houses. You know the saying: "Be it ever so humble, there is no place like home." So I have my own half-house, my property, thank God. Now, I ask you—what should I, a lonely widow with a child on her hands, want with a whole half-house? Isn't it enough for me to have just a tiny spot where I can lay my head? Especially when you have to make repairs to the house, and mend the roof, which hasn't been done for God knows how long. So my brother-in-law, Azriel, God bless him, keeps nagging me all the time: "Let's have the roof done, we need a new roof," he says. "All right," I says, "let's have the roof done." "So let's have it done then," he says. "All right, let's have it done." And so we went it backwards and forwards, roof here, roof there, but we didn't get anywhere. I don't have to tell you, that to have a roof done you need straw—lots of straw, to say nothing of the shingles. And where's the money to come from, I ask you? So I went and took in two lodgers; what else could I do? One room I let to Chaim-Chone, the deaf man—he's quite an old man already, a dodderer, one might say. His children pay me the rent—seventy kopeks a week—but he has his meals with them every other day. That is, one day he eats, one day he fasts, but even on the day he eats he half starves. He told me so himself. Maybe it isn't true, though, old people like to grumble, you know: however much you give them it's not enough, wherever you seat them it's no good, wherever you lay them it's hard.

What was I going to say? Oh, yes. You say: lodgers.... May God save you from them! I'm not saying anything about this deaf one—what can you expect from him? He's as quiet as a mouse. But when I let the other room to that flour-woman it was asking for trouble I was. Gnessy, her name is; she has a flour stall on the market. Yes, Gnessy. And what a plague of a woman! You should have seen how soft and sweet she was at first—honey couldn't be sweeter. It was "My darling, my dearie, I'll do this and that, I'll do anything for you." She doesn't need anything, she doesn't ask for anything. All she wants is that much room in the oven to put her pot in, and that much space at the edge of the board to salt and prepare the meat just once a week, and just a corner of the table to roll the dough out on once in a blue moon.

"And where are you going to keep your children, Gnessy?" I ask her. "You've got a whole brood of them, God bless 'em." "Don't you worry, darling," she says. "You don't know my children! They're not children, they're angels, they are. In the summer they're out in the street all day, and in winter they'll

crawl about on the top of the stove like kittens—
you won't ever hear them. The only trouble with them is
they are fond of eating, you can never give them enough
to eat." Ah, well, I suppose it's written that I've got to
suffer all my life. Some "angels," I tell you—one better
than the other! And so "clean"! A piece of bread alone
is not enough for them. And talk about noisy! The
screaming, the fighting, the yelling, the murder—it's hell.
Hell, did I say? Hell is a quiet place! But that's only
half the trouble. You can always quieten a child when
it comes to that—a kick, a pinch, a smack will do the
trick—after all, they're only children. But God blessed
her with a husband, too—Oizer, his name is. You ought
to know him, he's the *shammes* in the small synagogue,
a very pious Jew, and no fool, by the looks of it. But you
should see the way she treats him, that Gnessy—just
like dirt! "Oizer here, Oizer there! Oizer do this! Oizer
do that!" It's all you hear the livelong day: Oizer, Oizer.
And he! Just like water off a duck's back. He either jokes
it off (on top of all his woes he likes a joke) or else he
slaps his cap on the back of his head and walks out. He's
a lucky man to have such a good temper, I don't mind
telling you.

What was I going to say? Oh, yes. You say, bad lodgers. ... There are bad lodgers and bad lodgers! I'm not
the one to say anything against Gnessy, God forbid. She
isn't a spiteful cat, and she won't grudge a beggar a
crust of bread. But when she does get a fly in her nose,
then God help us! It's a disgrace, a scandal! I wouldn't
tell a living soul, I wouldn't, but between you and me—
sha, keep it a secret—she beats him, you know, on the
quiet. . . "Ah, Gnessy, Gnessy," I says to her, "you ought
to be ashamed of yourself, haven't you the fear of God?"
"Mind your own business!" she says. "Let the devil take
you," I says. "Let the devil take those who poke their
noses into other people's pots," she says. And I says, "Let

those go blind who have not seen anything better." And she says, "Let those become deaf who like to eavesdrop." Isn't she a shameless hussy!

What was I going to say? Oh, yes. You say, I love cleanliness.... I don't deny it, I like everything to be clean and spotless. What's wrong with it? But she doesn't like it, if you please. She can't stand it when my place is spick-and-span, and neat, and tidy. You ought to see her room! The dirt, the filth, mud up to your ears, the slop-pail always running over—*tfui*! First thing in the morning, before the children have rubbed their eyes open, the place is already topsyturvy. You call them children? They're devils! You can't compare them to my David, God bless him. My son David is all day in the *cheder*, and you won't find him doing nothing in the evenings either. He's either praying, or learning, or reading a book. But her brats! If they're not guzzling, they're yelling or fighting or just doing nothing. You follow me? I ask you, is it my fault if the Lord has blessed her with a bunch of mischievous little devils, and given me a jewel of a son, a boy of purest gold, may the Evil Eye spare him—I shed enough tears over him, God knows. What if I *am* a woman? A man in my place would never have stood it. Some men are a thousand times worse than women—I don't mean you. The moment life starts treating him a bit rough, he isn't a man any more. You don't have to look far for an example. Take, for instance, Yossel, Moisha-Avrom's son. So long as his wife Fruma-Necha was alive, all went well, but as soon as she died he cracked up, became a wet rag. "Yossel," I says to him, "pull yourself together, what can you do if a wife dies? It's God's will. How is it written in the scriptures?—'God giveth, God taketh.' I don't have to tell you that."

What was I going to say? Oh, yes. You say, an only son.... So he is, the only one I have. David, his name is. You don't know him? We named him David-Hersh, after my father-in-law. You should see him—the image of his father, may God prolong his life. Exactly like Moishe-Benzion, and the same face too—yellow, sickly, all skin and bones, and so weak, oh so weak! The *cheder* is too much for him, poor fellow. All those books, the Talmud and things. "You're killing yourself, Sonny, take it easy," I says. "Just look at yourself. Have something to eat, something to drink, have a glass of chicory," I says. "Chicory," he says, "you'd better drink yourself, Mother. You work so hard, you're killing yourself with work. Let me carry the basket from the market for you." "What are you talking about," I says. "What do you mean, carry baskets? My enemies" (I have plenty of them) "should not live to see it. You just sit there and learn." And I stand and look at him—the exact image of his father, may God preserve his soul; even the cough is the same. And does he cough, my God! It makes my heart bleed. I can't tell you how I suffered, what it cost me to put him on his feet! Let me tell you, Rabbi, no one believed he would live. There isn't an illness in the world that he didn't catch. You'd be surprised. If there was measles about—he caught it, if it was smallpox he got that too, if it was scarlet fever—he had scarlet fever, with diphtheria and tonsils and what not. God knows how many a night I sat up nursing him. God must have seen my tears, because He let me live to see the happy day when David celebrated his *Bar Mitzvah*. You think that was the end? You just listen: one winter evening, when he was coming home from *cheder*, he saw something white coming down the street flapping its arms. It doesn't take much to frighten a child, you know. He fainted away in the snow, and there he lay till someone found him and brought him home half dead. We had a job to bring him round, I tell you. And when we did bring him round, he was so ill that he was laid up with a high fever for six whole weeks. It's a wonder I lived through it. What I didn't do to save him! I made a solemn vow in the synagogue, I "sold" him and "bought" him back again, and gave him an extra name (Chaim-David-Hersh) so's the Angel of Death should not recognize him, and did I cry, did I shed tears! "O Heavenly Father," I prayed, "punish me, if you must, but don't take my only child away from me." And God must have heard my prayers, because my child began to get better. And then he says to me, "You know, Mother," he says. "I can give you regards from Father. He came to see me." When I heard that, I got such a nasty shock, my heart went tyoch-tyoch-tyoch. "Let him rest in peace," I says. "That's a sign that you will live long and enjoy good health." That's what I told him, but how I felt! Afterwards I found out who that thing in white with the flapping arms was. Do you know who it was, Rabbi? Guess. You are a learned clever man. Well, I'll tell you. It was Lipa, Lipa the water-carrier. He had bought himself a white sheepskin coat that day, and it being a bitter frost, he decided to warm himself up by flapping his arms, drat him. Such a muddle-head! Fancy a man putting on a white sheepskin coat all of a sudden!

What was I going to say? Oh, yes. You say, health. . . . Yes, health is the greatest blessing. That's what our doctor says, too, and he demands that I should feed my son up. Cook him a chicken broth every day, even if it be only a quarter of a chicken, if you can afford it. Feed him, he says, with milk and butter, and chocolate, if you can afford it. What does he mean—if you can afford it? As if there can be anything in the world I couldn't afford for my only son! If somebody told me, now: Go, Yenta, dig the earth, chop wood, carry water, knead clay, rob a church—for David's sake I'd do it even in the dead of night, in the sharpest frost. I would! Last summer he took it into his head that he wanted to read some books —textbooks he called them—I never set eyes on them in my life. But as I visit the houses of rich—on business, you know—he asked me if I could get those books for him and he gave me a list of the books, or textbooks, or whatever he called them. So I went to my houses and showed the list once, twice, but they all laughed at me. "What do you want those books for, Yenta? To feed your chickens and geese with?" All right, laugh, I says to myself. What do I care so long as my David has what to read. Well then, I got him those books, or textbooks, or whatever you call them, and night after night he read them and kept asking for more and more. I should worry! So I return the old ones and take new ones. And then that smart doctor comes along and asks, can I afford to cook a quarter of a chicken for David every day? And if three quarters of a chicken are needed, will I not do it? I ask you: where do such doctors come from? What kind of yeast are they raised on, and what kind of ovens are they baked in?

What was I going to say? Oh, yes. You say, chicken soup. . . . I cook a quarter of a chicken for him every day, I do, and give it to him in the evening when he comes home from *cheder*; he eats and I sit opposite with some work, feasting my eyes on him. And I pray to God that I may be able to cook him another quarter of a chicken the next day as well. "Mother," he says, "why don't you eat together with me?" "Eat in good health," I says, "I have eaten already." "What did you eat?" he asks. "I ate what I ate. You eat, you need it." But when he starts on his books, I go over to the oven, take out a couple of baked potatoes, or rub an onion on a piece of bread and have a feast. And believe me, or believe me not but I enjoy that onion more than the best pot roast. I'm so glad that David ate his soup and a quarter of a chicken, and that I have another quarter of a chicken prepared for the next day. The only trouble is he coughs so bad—whoo-whoo-whoo all the time. I says to the doctor, "Why don't you give him something for his cough," I says. And he says, "How old," he says, "was your husband Moishe-Benzion—may he rest in peace—when he died, and what did he die from?" I says: "He died," I says, "from death, that's what he died from. His time was up," I says, "so he died. What's his son got to do with it?"

Then he says, "I've got to know. I've examined your son. You have a fine son, a capable boy," he says. "Thank you for telling me," I says. "As if didn't know. Better give me some medicine for him, something to stop him coughing." "That's all very well," he says, "but you shouldn't let him sit over his books so long." "What then should he do?" I says. "Give him plenty to eat," he says, "and let him take walks every day. The main thing," he says, "don't let him sit nights over his books. If he *is* going to become a doctor," he says, "he wont miss it if he becomes one a few years later." I didn't like the way he talked at all. You could tell at once he was wrong in the head. Fancy saying that my David would become a doctor! He might as well have said he'd become a *gubernator*! When I came home I told David about it. He went all red and says, "You know what I'll tell you, Mother," he says. "Don't go to that doctor any more and don't speak to him," he says. "You won't catch me looking at him even," I says; "can't I see the man is not right in his head," I says. Who ever heard of a doctor being such a nosy parker asking his patients, what do you do for a living, how do you manage on it? What business is it of yours? You got your half a ruble? Well then, take it and write out the medicine!

What was I going to say? Oh, yes. You say, people have their hands full.... I should say so! So would you if you had a basket of eggs, and chickens, and ducks, and geese to run around with, and a couple of rich women who always want to be your first customer, in case, God forbid, the other one picks the best eggs and the best chickens. When, I ask you, can I find the time to cook soups, if I'm never at home? Yet I always find a way out. First thing in the morning, before I go to the market, I light a fire in the stove, salt the chicken, and run off, then I drop in for a minute, wash the meat, put the pot in the oven, and ask my lodger Gnessy to keep an eye on the pot, and when it boils, to cover it properly and put it on the embers. Not a difficult job, surely! How many times have I cooked a full supper for her! After all, we're only human beings, you know. We live among people, we don't live in the woods! And in the night, when I come home from work, I make a fire, and warm up the pot, and he has his chicken soup nice and hot and fresh. You'd think, now what could be better? But you forget that my lodger is a—I'd rather not say what she is, damn her. This morning she took it into her head to cook a dairy breakfast for those brats of hers—dumplings with milk. I don't understand what taste there is in those dumplings! And why all of a sudden a Sabbath meal on an ordinary weekday? A funny woman, if you ask me! Sometimes she doesn't make a fire for days, then all of a sudden, here you are! She cooks a big pot of groats, or grits, or God knows what it is—you have to put on spectacles to find a grain in it, and even then you won't find anything. Sometimes she cooks a pot of fish-potatoes that's really all onion—you can smell it a mile off—not to mention pepper—she loves pepper, she does—and all day they run about with their mouths open, gasping for breath and blowing, "Hua! Hua!"

What was I going to say? Oh, yes. You say: unlucky.... So my lodger takes it into her head to make buckwheat dumplings, and she puts a crock of milk on the stove to boil. Her children went mad for joy. You'd think they had never tasted milk in all their lives. And you should have seen the amount of milk there was—may our enemies have as much—maybe two spoonfuls at the most, the rest was all water. But for a poor man it was a feast! At that moment, who the devil should come blundering in but the *shammes*. He must have smelled that rich meal in the synagogue, because he came running in, as always, with a joke: "Good *yom-tev* everybody!" And she comes back with: "What the devil of a holiday is it? What's brought you here so early?" "I was afraid to miss the Grace," he says. "What have you got there in the oven?" "Something specially for you," she says, "a big fig in a little pot!" "Why not a big pot?" he says. "It would then be enough for the two of us." "Oh," she says, "go to the devil with your jokes!" and she grabs the oven-fork to get the crock of milk out of the oven, but the crock turns over and the milk spills all over the oven. And that started it! Gnessy cursed her husband, called him all the names you could think of. Lucky for him he took his foot in his hand and cleared out in good time. Those brats of hers tumbled down from the stove screaming and wailing as if their father and mother had been murdered. "May your dumplings and milk be damned," I says. "Because of them my David's soup may be spoilt. My pot isn't *kosher* any more!" "To hell with your pot!" she says. "All my dumplings and milk are dearer to me than all your pots and all the soups you stuff into that David of yours." "You know what," I says, "your whole brood of brats is not worth my son's little finger-nail!" "You know what," she says, "I spit on that David of yours. He's just one, and look how many I have got." Such a hussy as that Gnessy has not been seen in all the world! For words like that she ought to have her mouth lashed with a wet rag!

What was I going to say? Oh, yes. You say, dairy things and meat things should not be kept in the same oven. That's just what happened. The crock turned over and if any of that milk, God forbid, touched my chicken pot, then I am done for. As a matter of fact I don't see how the milk could possibly have reached my pot, because it was standing way over in a corner of the oven with the hot ash all round it. Mind you, I couldn't swear to it, though. Still, you never know. It's such a pity, David won't have anything to eat. But maybe I'll think up something for him. As it happens I brought some geese from the butcher yesterday and prepared them for my customers; naturally I left myself some of the giblets for the Sabbath. At a pinch I could make something out of them. But the trouble is, I have no other pot. If, God forbid, Rabbi, you decide that my pot is not *kosher* any more, I'll be left without a pot. And without a pot I am as without an arm, as I only have one pot. As a matter of fact, I had three pots before, but that Gnessy, damn her, borrowed a pot from me, a brand-new pot it was, and goes and returns me a cracked pot. "Whose pot is this?" I says. And she says, "What do you mean, it's your pot." So I says, "How can it be my pot, when I gave you a new pot and this pot is cracked?" So she says, "*Sha*, you needn't shout, you can't scare me. For one thing, I gave you back a good pot; secondly, when I took the pot from you it was cracked already; and thirdly, I never took any pot from you at all, I have my own pot, and leave me alone, let me be!" What do you think of her?

What was I going to say? Oh, yes. You say, an extra pot in the house always comes in useful. ... So I was left with only two good pots and one cracked pot, which is as good as saying that I had only two pots left. But can a poor person have such a luxury as two pots? One day I came back from the market with a basketful of chickens, and the cat goes and frightens those chickens for me. You ask: where did I get a cat? That was another of her ideas—hers and those brats of hers. They found a kitten somewhere and started tormenting the poor thing. "Have pity on the kitten," my David tells them, "it's a living being!" But what do they care, those idlers and ruffians! To make a long story short, they went and tied something to the kitten's tail, and the kitten began to chase round like mad, frightening my chickens, and one of them got undone and flew up on the top shelf—and bang! over went a pot. You think it was the cracked pot that fell? No such luck! If a pot has to be broken it will always be a new pot! It's been like that from the beginning of time. I wonder why? For instance, here are two people walking along. One walks, and the other walks. One of them is his mother's one and only, the apple of her eye, the other one, say, is.... Rabbi! Good God, what's the matter with you! Rabbi! Where is your wife? Where is she! Hurry up! Quick! The rabbi feels bad! He's fainting! Water, water!

1901

ADVICE

"SOME YOUNG man has been asking for you these last three days. He comes every day, morning and evening. Says he wants to see you badly."

This glad news was communicated to me when I returned home once after a journey.

"No doubt some young author with a novel," I thought.

As soon as I sat down to the desk and began working the bell rang.

I could hear the street door being opened, someone moving about in the hall. Taking off his galoshes. Coughing. Blowing his nose. By all signs an author. I was getting quite keen to see the fellow. At last, with God's help, he enters my room. He greets me most politely. To be more exact, he makes an elaborate bow, and, rubbing his hands, introduces himself. He gives his name—one of those names that have a habit of instantly slipping your memory.

"Sit down," I say. "What can I do for you?"

"I have come to see you on a highly important matter. In other words, the business I have come to see you on is extremely important to me. I will say more—it is a matter of life and death. I think you will grasp what it is right away. After all, you are a writer, you write a good deal, and therefore you know what's what. Yes, that's what I think—that is, I don't even think it, I am sure of it...."

I glance at my visitor. He is a typical small-town educator, and obviously an "author." He is a young man with a pale face and mournful black eyes which seem to plead: "Have pity on a lost and lonely soul!"

I don't like such eyes. I am afraid of them. There is never a spark of laughter or a smile in them. Definitely, I don't like such eyes.

I lay my pen down and say to the author, "Well, let's see what you have there?" I expect my visitor to dive into his pocket and fish out a bulky manuscript. It may be a novel in three parts—as long as the Jewish Exile. The chances are that it is a drama in four acts. And the characters in the play will have names like Murderson, Erlichman, Frumhartz and Bitterzweig, names that tell you in advance exactly whom you have to do with.

On the other hand the author might have brought neither a novel nor a play, but just a verse about Zion:

> *In the hills lies his quest,*
> *Where the eagle builds its nest,*
> *And the palms there blossom best;*
> *There the prophets come to rest*
> *And all the land by God is blest.*

Such verses are all too familiar to me. Too well do I know those rhymes, which grate on your ears and make dots and circles dance before your eyes. A black despondency floods one's soul after the reading of such verses.

But, just imagine—I was mistaken. The young man did not dive under his jacket and fish from thereunder any manuscript. He had no intention of reading me his novel. Instead, he adjusted his collar, cleared his throat, and said:

"Well, as a matter of fact, I have come here to pour out the bitterness of my heart to you. I will say more: I have come to ask your advice. I think that a person like you, a man who writes, ought to be able to understand me, and consequently, be in a position to give me good advice. And believe me, I will do whatever you tell me. I can give you my word of honour, if you like. But, pardon me, perhaps I am taking up your time?"

I feel as if a load has been taken off my mind, and it is in the most amiable of tones that I say to the man who brought no manuscript, "Time does not count. Tell me what your trouble is."

My visitor draws his chair up closer to the desk and proceeds slowly to pour out the bitterness of his heart. He starts off calmly, working himself up gradually as he goes along.

"Well, you should know that I come from a small town. As a matter of fact, our town is not such a small one. I should rather say it was a large town, a city almost. But in comparison with your town our town is a small town. Of course, you know our town very well. But I will not disclose its name to you, because you might want to describe it, for all I know. And that doesn't suit me for various reasons. I suppose you would like to know what my occupation is? Ahem. . . . My occupation—Well, up till now I have not been doing anything. I am still 'sitting' at the expense of my father-in-law and mother-in-law. That's to say, we live together, because she's their only daughter, they have no other children. They can afford it. They can keep us another ten years, they are well-to-do people. If you like to know, they are rich. For a small town like ours I should say they are very rich. In a word, they're the richest people we have. Of course, you must have heard about my father-in-law. But I don't intend to reveal his name to you. It wouldn't do. Between you and me, though, he likes to have himself talked about. For instance, he made a bigger donation than anyone else for the benefit of those who suffered in the Bobruisk fire. For the town of Kishinev, too, he gave more than anyone else. But for our own town he gives practically nothing. Other towns—yes, he likes to be talked about. He is no fool: he knows perfectly well that he is very much looked up to in our town as it is. So why should he pretend to be liberal and show off before no one knows who? When anyone comes to him with a petition or for alms he goes as white as a ghost. He shouts at them, 'Aha! You've come to rob me, have you? Here, take my keys! Go and rummage in my wardrobes. Take all I have!' Perhaps you think that he really gives his keys? Pardon me, but you are mistaken. The keys of his wardrobes are locked up in his desk. And the key of his desk is hidden away, too, in a safe place. That's the kind of man my father-in-law is. But then he admits it himself that he simply can't bring himself to give people anything. That's why people in our town call him a swine—behind his back, of course. Between you and me, he has fully earned that name. Generally speaking, though, people flatter him to his face. And what flattery—it's enough to make you sick. But he likes it and takes it for granted. Pats his tummy and feels on top of the world. Ah, that is the life! Now I ask you—what more can a man want? He does nothing, he lives on the fat of the land, he eats well, sleeps well. What more can a man want? After a good nap he orders his phaeton and goes out for a little drive through the mud. And in the evening he has guests coming. Nearly all of them leading men of the town. They gossip, chatter nonsense, make fun of all the townspeople and everybody in the world. Then a big samovar is served up. And here my father-in-law sits down to a game of dominoes with the *shochet*

Shmuel-Abeh. Shmuel-Abeh the *shochet*, you should know, is a young man with side ringlets, but a modern young man in a white collar, and polished boots, who doesn't run away from young women, who can sing well, can read a newspaper and play a good game of chess and dominoes. They can play dominoes, you should know, all night long, while you have to sit there and watch them, yawning fit to dislocate your jaws. You'd much rather get up from the table and go into your own room to read a book or a newspaper, but you dare not. To leave the room, you see, isn't proper. My father-in-law doesn't like it. He doesn't say anything, just gets sulky, puffs himself up like an old turkey, and doesn't speak to you. My mother-in-law takes her cue from him, and looks on you as if you were dirt. And once the parents are at odds with their son-in-law, then their offspring, too, as the saying goes, turns her nose up. That offspring, let me tell you, has a high opinion of herself. No wonder—she's the "apple of their eye," and when she doesn't feel well they send at once for the doctor and the whole world goes topsyturvy. No wonder—she thinks the world has been created specially for her. Between you and me, though, if she isn't exactly a downright fool, she's none too clever. As a matter of fact, when she speaks you wouldn't notice that she's foolish. On the contrary, she strikes you as being rather clever than foolish. Sometimes she might even strike you as being extremely clever. But what's the good of being clever when she is as spoilt and pampered as a wild goat? She does nothing all day long but laugh or cry. And when she does cry, it's like a little baby. Sometimes you ask her, 'What are you crying for? What haven't you got?' The wall would answer you sooner than she would. This wouldn't be so bad—a wife cries till she cries herself out. The worst of it is she cries so loud that the mother-in-law comes running in. Comes in with her Turkish shawl on her shoulders. Wrings her hands. Cries out in a prayerful voice. And her voice, you should know, is gruff, like a man's. She asks her child, 'What's the matter, daughter dear? Him again?' No answer. Then, looking at me, she cries out: 'Ah, it's that robber of yours again, the bandit, the murderer! What does he care that I have a one and only child, the only eye in my head? He didn't suffer, he didn't bleed!' And out come tumbling the words, just like dried peas out of a sack. I feel so wretched, so sick at heart, that a sudden mad desire seizes me to snatch off that Turkish shawl of hers, crush it in my hands, dance on it, tear it up into shreds. Sanely speaking, though, the shawl has nothing to do with it, of course. Just a shawl as shawls go, one of the kind that are usually brought from Brod. I suppose you know those Turkish shawls? You know that check pattern with the dark spots and a fringe...."

At this point I interrupt my young visitor sternly:

"Excuse me, but you wanted to see me on business, I believe. You have come to ask me for my advice."

The visitor heaves a deep sigh. "Oh, I'm sorry," he says, "maybe I'm taking up your time? But all this is so important—all what I am telling you. I must give you some idea of the house and its tenants. Only then will you really understand my position and what it's all about. Well then, in comes my mother-in-law in that Turkish shawl of hers. And she takes it into her head for some reason that that precious child of hers is ailing. This is where my father-in-law takes matters in hand. He orders out the phaeton and sends for the doctor. He sends for the "new doctor"—that's what they call one of the doctors in our town, damn him. But I won't reveal his name to you for various reasons. And here is where it begins, the thing I came to tell you about and get your advice on."

My visitor pauses for a minute. He mops his perspiring face with his handkerchief and moves closer up to me with his chair in preparation for resuming his story. Meanwhile he picks up some object from my desk. There are people who cannot speak unless they hold something in their hands. And my desk has all kinds of knick-knacks on it, among them a cigar-cutter in the shape of a tiny bicycle. My visitor seemed to have taken a fancy to the thing. When starting his story he had merely glanced at the bicycle, then he had picked it up and begun to turn the little wheels. The thing was in his hands practically all the time he was speaking.

"So they send for the new doctor," he goes on. "And in our little town, let me tell you, doctors are as plentiful as stray dogs. We have Russian doctors, and Jewish doctors, and Zionist doctors, but the doctor I am telling you about is a different kind of doctor altogether. He is a young local doctor, the son of a tailor. He's no longer a tailor, of course. Why should he be when his son is a doctor? Or rather—why should a doctor-son have a tailor-father? Just a word about the father to give you some idea of him. He is a squint-eyed man of absolutely short stature, with a crooked finger on his right hand. He goes about always in a long quilted gaberdine. And he has a voice like a *grager*—a chatterbox. Day and night he goes about chattering about his son: 'My son's a doctor. Yesterday he saw a patient.... He can do anything.... He has a practice....' Yes, that tailor buzzes his son's fame about all over the town. And the worst of it is that that son of his is a women's doctor. In other words, an obstetrician. And if anyone has a secret in that respect, you may be sure that tailor will trumpet it all over the town. In short, woe to that woman or girl who falls into the hands of that doctor or his tailor-father. There was a girl in our town, who—"

Again I interrupt my visitor.

"Excuse me, young man, but you wanted to see me on some business, I believe."

"Oh, I'm sorry," he says, "am I taking up your time? But how can I not tell you about the tailor, when that tailor is my evil genius! If not for that doctor, things would have gone swimmingly with me. Judge for yourself—what more do I need? I have a beauty of a wife, clever as can be, the only child of her parents, and we have no children of our own. In a hundred and twenty years or so, when they die, all their wealth and honours will become hers, that is, mine. Even now—*tfui-tfui*, touch wood—I enjoy a certain amount of respect. When I'm a guest at table anywhere, they always give me a seat of honour as the son-in-law of a rich man. During the synagogue service at *Succos* I always go first after my father-in-law. Well, not exactly first, maybe, but after the cantor and the rabbi. And only then all the rest. Even, excuse me, at the baths, I am treated the same way. I've hardly had time to undress, when the bath-house attendant shouts out, 'Hi, there, people, make way! Stand clear of the doors! The son-in-law of our rich man is going to have a bath!' No, the words of the bath-house attendant are not pleasing to me, I don't like such attentions. It's all very well to say I don't like! Who doesn't like flattery, who rejects honours? But only I know how little I deserve it. Just because my father-in-law is a rich man? People can lick him if they like it. What is it to me? Savages, I tell you, just savages! And I have to sit with them just like in a prison. I can't meet people of my own level because it isn't the proper thing for the son-in-law of a rich man, and to talk to my father-in-law is simply impossible. For that matter—what *is* my father-in-law? He can't hear me, so I may as well tell you—he's an ignoramus! There's nothing to speak to him about. And she, their only daughter, is just a wild goat—either she laughs all the time or suddenly throws herself down on her bed and sobs.

And then, as I told you, my father-in-law sends the phaeton for the new doctor, may he roast in hell! Ah, believe me, when I think of that doctor life becomes unbearable to me! At such moments I feel like grabbing a knife and cutting my throat or running down to the river and drowning myself in it!"

The young man grew thoughtful and sad.

At this point, choosing my words carefully, I ask my visitor:

"Am I to understand, then, that you suspect this doctor, that he ... and your wife. ..."

My visitor leaps from his chair as if he has been scalded.

"Heaven forbid!" he cries. "I have no such suspicions. Goodness, no! After all, she's a Jewish daughter! A pious child! I speak of the doctor, may he burn in Gehenna! And may the same fire devour his father, that squint-eyed tailor, who noses around in his quilted gaberdine! Noses around, and jabbers, and babbles all over the town. You'd think—who listens to him? The man talks piffle, tommy-rot! I wouldn't think any more of it than I would of last year's snow, but people have ears, and ears like to listen, and if you listen well enough, you can hear things you would be the happier for not having heard. But you've got to know our little town. It's famous the world over for the number of gossips and long-tongued scandalmongers it has. I will say more: If a man gets caught on their tongues, he may as well go and drown himself. Now you just asked me—do I suspect this doctor? No, I had no suspicions of him. But after all that gossip I nevertheless started to keep my eyes and ears open. I was careful not to miss a word of his whenever he spoke to her. But I saw nothing suspicious in their conduct or conversation. But what I did notice was that she becomes quite a different person when she sees him. Her face changes, her eyes change. A kind of sparkle suddenly comes into her eyes. And her face takes on a different expression to the one she has when I am there. Yes, I asked her once, 'Tell me, my sweet, why is it you become quite a different person when he calls?' You'll never guess what she answered me. She didn't answer me at all. She just laughed, such a withering laugh I thought I would die! Then she threw herself on her bed in a fit of sobbing and fainted away. Naturally, in came running my mother-in-law in that Turkish shawl of hers, and started trying to bring her round, while my father-in-law ordered the phaeton and sent me this time for the new doctor. And when I brought the doctor she suddenly felt better. Her eyes began to sparkle again, like brilliants in the sun, and little roses came out in her cheeks. Can you imagine my position! I had to go for him to his home and bring him back to mine in the phaeton. It would have been easier for me, maybe, to have walked into hell than to walk into that place where he lived and to look at that face of his—some face! Red like a boiled crab's, with pimples all fighting for a place on it. And he has a habit, that doctor, of grinning like a carp when he has to and doesn't have to. He is honey itself, smooth and soft as a sticking-plaster over a boil. An angel could not have been nicer to me. The other day, when I caught that fashionable disease they call the influenza, he laid himself out so hard to cure me that I felt uncomfortable. The surprising thing is—the nicer he is towards me the more I hate him. May God forgive me for saying so, but I can't bear the sight of him. Especially when he sits with us and he and she exchange those glances between them. I feel then as if I could take him by the scruff of his neck and throw him out. I'd feel better for it. All the same, sir, I have sworn to put an end to it. I've had enough of his honeyed little smiles and his glances when he comes to us and sits next to her. How long, I ask you, can a man stand the shame of it? The gossips and scandalmongers of our town have been at me for a long time now. No, I have definitely made up my mind to divorce her. There's no other way. On the other hand the question arises: that's all very well, but what do I gain by divorcing her? When all is said and done, my father-in-law is a rich man, she's an only daughter, all theirs will be mine. Then comes the thought: But how did I manage before? And what do other young people do? Oh, damn it, I'll divorce her, there's no other way. Eh? What do you say?"

My visitor draws his breath, mops his face, and looks at me timidly, waiting for my reply. I say:

"That's what I think, too. There is no other way out for you. What's more, your love is anything but ardent. And you have no children. And the town is gossiping. What do you want it for?"

My visitor is busy turning the wheels of the toy bicycle as he listens to my reply, gazing at me with those mournful have-pity-on-me eyes of his. Then he moves up still closer, heaves a painful sigh and begins again:

"You say—love. I can't say that I detest her—why should I detest her? Naturally I love her. As a matter of fact, I love her very much. As for the town gossiping, let them gossip if they like it. No, sir, the fire that burns within me comes from other causes. The one thing I can't bear is that she is so glad to see the doctor. I ask you: now why doesn't she get pink and gay when she sees me? In what way am I any worse than he? Because he's a doctor and I'm not? If I had been taught I'd have become a doctor, too. And maybe a better doctor than he is. Believe me, he's not a patch on me when it comes to Hebrew learning. These thoughts somewhat shake my resolution. Why should I divorce her? Because of that new doctor? What would I do if in place of the new doctor there came some other black devil? Where does it stand written that a young woman must not be acquainted with a doctor? That's one thing. Secondly, I ask you—what will become of me if I divorce her? When all is said and done I'm just an orphan, without relatives, without friends. It's easy for you to say—divorce her. Well, I divorce her, say—and then where should I be? Back again where I was—a poor lad, who has to begin life all over again and start marrying someone again. And how do I know that I'll find me a better wife than she is? What if I land in a worse hell than what I've been living in till now? At least here I've got used to it, so to say, and I know what I'm in for. When it comes to that, the headache I have here is the headache of a crown prince who will step into a fortune. In a hundred years that fortune will be hers, that is, mine. So why should I start making combinations and speculations, so to speak. And life, you know, is a gamble, a lottery. Eh? Isn't that so? Don't you think it's a lottery?"

I answer my visitor:

"To some extent it is a gamble, a lottery. If that's how you feel about it, it *would* be better not to divorce her, and make it up between you."

I thought this a good piece of advice, which definitely settled the whole business on a peaceful footing. For a moment I even thought the conversation with my visitor was drawing to an end. But I was sadly mistaken. My visitor pounces on the toy bicycle again, starts turning the wheels and says, looking me straight in the face:

"You say—make it up with her? But what about the doctor, may the devil tear him limb from limb! And the doctor's father—that squint-eyed tailor? As it is, the fellow trumpets it about all over the town that the daughter of my father-in-law is going to divorce me! What do you think of such meanness? Have you ever heard such filthy gossip as that scoundrelly tailor goes about spreading? On the other hand, I ask myself: once the whole town now knows it, then what do I lose in that case? Absolutely nothing. Pardon the aphorism: a broken plate can't be more broken than it is. On the other hand, though, once my divorce is the talk of the town, is it seeming for me to defy those opinions? No, sir, there is no other way out for me except a divorce. Eh? Isn't that so? What do you say?"

"Perhaps you are right," I answer. "Once your divorce is the talk of the town it does seem a bit awkward for you to go against it."

My visitor bears down on me chair and all and shouts:

"Aha! Then, according to you, I must give her a divorce at all cost! No, sir, you've got to give the matter careful consideration before jumping to conclusions. Say you were a rabbi and I come to you with my wife to get a divorce. Naturally, you ask me, 'Tell me, young man, what is the reason why you want to divorce your wife?' Now what answer, for instance, should I give the rabbi? Must I answer him, according to you, 'She looks at the doctor and he at her?' Is there any sense in such an answer? But what else *can* I answer? I can't very well cover up their eyes, can I? And what will I look like, what will the world think of me, if I divorce her because of that? Why, everyone will say the man's gone mad, divorcing a beauty of a wife at the very moment when their whole fortune will be hers, that is, mine in a hundred odd years! That's what you would say too—yes, you are mad. Eh? Wouldn't you?"

"So I would—stark-staring mad."

My visitor has moved up so close that our legs are almost entwined. Throwing aside the toy bicycle, which was now spoilt, my visitor lays hold of my inkwell. He draws a deep breath and plunges on:

"It's all very well for you to say I've gone mad. I'd like to see what you would do if you had had this happen to you? Now just think for a minute: your father-in-law is an ignoramus, your mother-in-law goes about in a Turkish shawl and grumbles in a masculine voice, your wife, God bless her, has a doctor attending her all the time, and the whole town pokes its finger at you and says behind your back, 'There goes the young cuckold!' Why, you'd jump out of bed in the middle of the night and run away to the place where black pepper grows! Eh? What? Wouldn't you?"

I tell my visitor:

"Yes, that is so. I daresay I would jump out of bed in the middle of the night, divorce her and run away to the place where black pepper grows."

My visitor shouts at me:

"It's all very well for you to say: jump out of bed, divorce her, and run away to where black pepper grows! Run! Why run? Who runs? Where runs? To the grave? You just think a moment, man: she's an only daughter. In a hundred odd years all that is theirs will be mine! Is that nothing to you? When all is said and done—what have I got against her? No, really, ask me, what have I got against her?"

"Really," I ask my visitor, "what have you got against her?"

In reply my visitor yells in a frenzy:

"What do you mean—what? And the doctor? Have you forgotten the doctor? So long as that hyena hangs about the place I can't bear to look at her."

"Oh yes," I say. "The doctor! Well, in that case you must divorce her."

"And what do I gain by it?" shouts my visitor. "Let's say I divorce her—all right. And what am I going to do with myself in these hard times? No, don't try to twist out of it. You are a clever Jew."

"I think you ought not to divorce her," I say.

"Not divorce her? But what about the doctor? So long as he—"

I want to put an end to our conversation and so I say in a firm tone:

"Divorce her."

"But what will I gain by it?"

"Then don't divorce her."

"What about the doctor?"

I don't know, dear reader, what exactly happened to me. It must have been a rush of blood to the head or something. Whatever it was, I caught my visitor by the throat, pushed him up against the wall and yelled in a voice not like my own:

"Divorce her! Give her a divorce, imbecile! A divorce! A divorce! A divorce!"

My whole family came running in at the noise. What's up? What's the matter?

Why, nothing. Everything's all right.

But when I looked in the mirror and saw my deathly pale face I got a shock.

Holding my visitor's hand, I kept begging his pardon and asking him to forget what had happened. I said to him:

"You know how it is, sometimes a man just loses his temper for no apparent reason."

My visitor was utterly confused and bewildered, and agreed with everything I said. He agreed that a man was not master of himself and sometimes he really did lose his temper.

And my visitor took his leave of me the same way as he had come in—rubbing his hands and bowing politely and respectfully.

"I am sorry to have taken up so much of your time," he said before going. "Thank you very much for your advice. Good-day! Be well."

"Don't mention it. I wish you a happy journey."

1904

THE LUCKIEST MAN IN KODNO

o you know what the best time is to travel by
train? In the autumn, shortly after the *Succos* holidays.
It isn't hot, and it isn't cold. You don't see the tearful
sky or the dark mournful earth. The pattering raindrops
roll down the misty window-panes like tears. But you
sit in your third-class carriage like a lord in the company
of other aristocrats like yourself, and glance out of the
window from time to time. Somewhere far out you see a
cart trundling through the mire. On the cart, bent up almost double with a sack over his head, sits one of God's
creatures, venting his rage on another of God's creatures—the poor little horse. And you praise the Lord for
having a roof over your head and the companionship of
living souls. I don't know about you, but personally I'm
very fond of travelling by train in the autumn, shortly
after the *Succos* holidays.

The main thing for me is the seat. If I manage to get
hold of a seat, and that seat is on the right side next to
the window, then I feel myself a king. You get out your
cigarette case, light a cigarette, and smoke one after the
other, while you look round to see who you are travelling
with and whether there's anyone you can have a chat

with. The passengers, thank God, are like herrings in a barrel. Beards, noses, caps, bellies—all in the images of men, but not a man amongst them. Wait a minute, though—who is that strange creature sitting over there in the corner all by himself? He looks like none of the rest. I have an eye for that kind of thing. I'll pick out a peculiar person among hundreds.

To look at him he might have been just an ordinary man, an "everyday Jew," as they say with us—one of those who go twelve to the dozen. But his dress was rather peculiar. You couldn't tell whether it was a gaberdine he had on or a capote, a hat on his head or a skull-cap, an umbrella in his hand or a besom. Very odd attire!

But it was the man himself who was arresting, not his clothes. He just couldn't sit still, and kept fidgeting and looking round from side to side, while his face fairly glowed with joy and happiness.

You could swear the man had drawn a big winner, or had had the good luck to see his daughter married, or maybe his son fixed up in the gymnasium. He kept jumping up every minute, looking out of the window and saying to himself, "Station? No?" Then he'd sit down again, every time closer and closer to me, all radiant, joyous, happy.

I don't mind telling you that I'm not that nosy kind who like to pry into other people's souls and worm out the why and wherefore. I just go my way, and if a man has anything on his mind he'll tell you himself.

And so it was. We hadn't passed two stations before that beaming man was sitting right next to me, so close, in fact, that his mouth almost touched my nose.

"Where does a Jew travel?" he asked.

Judging by the question, by the way he scratched his head and by everything else about him, I could see that he was not so much interested to know where I was going as he was eager to tell me where he was going himself. And so I obliged him by not answering his question, but asking him in turn, "And where are you?"

And off he went.

"Where I am going? To Kodno. Have you heard of Kodno? I am a Kodno man. It's not far from here. The third stop. That's to say, another three stations from here. That's right! And from there it's another hour and a half by horse and cart. But that's only a way of talking—an hour and a half. As a matter of fact it takes two full hours and a good bit extra—that's if the road is good and you are travelling by carriage. I have already ordered one by telegraph, I sent a telegram to have a phaeton sent down to the station. For myself, you think? Don't you worry, I can ride sixth in an ordinary *balagula* cart if it comes to that. And if not, I just take my umbrella in one hand, my bundle in the other, and foot it. We can't afford phaetons, you see. Business with us is so good that I might just as well sit at home altogether. Eh? What did you say?"

Here my companion makes a pause, sighs, then goes on again, lowering his voice, and speaking close to my ear, after a preliminary look round to see that nobody was listening.

"I am not by myself. I am travelling with a professor.... What have I to do with a professor? It's a story. Have you ever heard of Kashevarovka? There is a little town by that name—Kashevarovka they call it. Well, there's a rich Jew living there, an upstart, maybe you've heard of him—Borodenko, Itzik Borodenko. How do you like the name? A real Russian handle! But what difference does a name make—whether Russian or Jewish—so long as he has the money? And that he has, lots of it. In a word, that man is valued with us in Kodno at half a million. And if you insist on it very much, I'll agree with you even that he's worth a full million. Judging, excuse me, by his piggishness, he may be worth two millions. Let me show you. Although I've never met you before, I see that you travel about a lot more than I do. Well then, tell me truly—have you ever heard of this Borodenko proving himself to be a real good Jew, making some big donation or anything of that kind? So far we people in Kodno don't seem to have heard anything about it. However, I am not God's advocate, and everyone would like to go partners with someone else's pocket. But I am not talking about charity and donations, I am talking about ordinary human kindness. With God's help you have become so rich that you can afford to send for a professor, so why should you mind if another person took advantage of the opportunity through you? No one is asking you for money, all they ask for is you should put in a good word, so what devil is with you! You just listen.

"It had to happen that we in Kodno got to know (we in Kodno know everything) that a daughter of Kashevarovka's rich man, that is, Itzik Borodenko I was telling you about, had fallen ill. And what do you think was the matter with her? Bah, a mere nothing—just a love affair. She fell in love with a Russian lad and the lad spurned her, so she went and took poison (we in Kodno know everything). That happened only yesterday. They rushed off at once and got a professor down for her, the most famous of all the professors. What is it to such a rich man! Well, it occurred to me that this professor wouldn't stay there for ever. If not today, then tomorrow, but he would have to go back. And going back he would have to pass our station, Kodno, that is. So why shouldn't he drop in at my place from one train to another? You see, my child is laid up. Something wrong inside. He doesn't cough, thank God, and it isn't his heart either. Then what's wrong with him? There isn't a drop of blood in his face, and he's weak, weak as a fly. And all because he doesn't eat. Not a crumb. Absolutely nothing. Sometimes he'll have a glass of milk, and even then he has to force himself to drink it; you have to go down on your knees and beg him. And nothing more. Not a spoon of soup, not a crumb of bread. As for meat, that's out of the question. He can't stand meat, just can't stomach it. He's been like that ever since he had the blood come from his throat. Last summer that was. It only happened once, it's true, but it was pretty bad. He doesn't have it any more, thank God. But he's so weak, I can't tell you. He can hardly stand on his legs. It's no joke, running a boiling temperature like a man with the smallpox. It's been a hundred and three ever since *Shevuos*, and nothing helps. I've been to the doctor with him time and again. But what do they know, those doctors of ours? Give him more to eat, they say, and plenty of air. It's all very well to say more to eat when he doesn't want to eat at all. As for air, where have we got air? Air in Kodno? Ha, ha! A nice little place, Kodno, a real Jewish little town. We have here, praise God, Jews, a synagogue, a *Bes Hamedresh*, a rabbi, and all the rest of it. There are only two things God has not blessed us with—the means of earning a living and air. Well, about a living, what can I tell you? We make a living, thank God, one from the other. But as for air— When we want air we go to the manor grounds for it. There's lots of air at the manor, I don't mind telling you. Before, when Kodno used to belong to the Polish *pans*, you daren't show your nose at the manor. The *pans* would not let you come near it. But ever since the Kodno manor has passed into the hands of Jews, the dogs have gone, and the manor itself is not what it used to be. It's a pleasure to go there. There are *pans* there now, too—landowners, but they are Jewish landowners. They speak Jewish like you and me. They keep Jewish customs and treat Jews decently. In a word, they are real Jews. I shouldn't say they are very pious, though. They are in no great hurry to come to our synagogue, still less to our bath-house. They have no qualms about breaking the *Shabbas* law either. And it's no great sin with them to roast a chicken in butter. As for cutting the beard and going with the head uncovered and suchlike things—it goes without saying: it has become the usual thing these days. Even in Kodno we have smart fellows whose caps are too heavy for their heads. Yes, Kodno can't complain about its landowners. Our Jewish *pans* treat the town well, try to show themselves at their best. In the autumn they send down a hundred or so sacks of potatoes for the poor, in the winter they provide straw for heating, before Passover they give money to buy flour for *matzos*. Not long ago they made a present of bricks to build a new synagogue. To be sure! Everything right and proper and decent. If only it wasn't that chicken roasted in butter! That's too bad! I don't want you to think I'm trying to run them down altogether. On the contrary, I've got nothing but good to say of them. And they wouldn't exchange me for a sip of *borshch* either. Why, if you want to know, Reb Alter (Reb Alter—that's me) is quite a personage with them, you might say. Whenever they need something there in town—a calendar, say, for the new year, or *matzos* for Passover, or willow branches for the *Succos* festival and suchlike things required by Jewish custom, they send at once for Reb Alter. And they spend a lot of money in my wife's shop too (my wife keeps a little shop) on salt, and pepper, and matches and what not. That's the landowners themselves. As for their children, the young students—they think the world of my son. When they come down from St. Petersburg for the summer they teach 'mine' all kinds of things; they sit poring over books with him for days on end. And 'mine,' let me tell you, would give his life for a book, and his mother's and father's too. If you ask me, it was books that ruined him. Books started the whole trouble. 'She' tries to make out that it was the conscription that started it. But what has the conscription got to do with it? That business was all done with and forgotten. Well, anyway, whatever it was, whether books or conscription, the fact remains that my son is wasting away, melting, poor lad, like a candle. Only God can help him."

For a minute his radiant face clouded, but only for a minute. The sun peeped out again and drove the cloud away, and once more his face beamed, his eyes sparkled and his mouth smiled. Presently he was continuing his story again.

"Well, where were we? Ah yes! So I thought to myself —I'll run down to Kashevarovka and see that rich man, Itzik Borodenko. Naturally, I did not start on my journey just like that, with empty hands, as the saying goes. I provided myself with a letter, you understand. A letter from our rabbi (our Kodno rabbi is known far and wide, you know). A wonderful letter! 'Since the Lord hath blessed thy house with plenty and thou canst afford to call thee out a professor; and since our Reb Alter's son, God guard thee, is lying on his deathbed—will not a spark of mercy be kindled in thy heart, and wilt thou not graciously condescend to put thyself in his place; perhaps thou wilt succeed in persuading the professor to visit us if only for a quarter of an hour on his way back, from one train to another—he is passing Kodno in any case— to examine the sick boy. May the Lord bless thee for this act of human kindness. . . .' And so on. A wonderful letter!"

All of a sudden the train hooted and stopped. My companion sprang to his feet.

"Aha! A station! I'll just pop in to the first-class carriage for a moment. I'll just take a look at my professor and come back and finish my story."

He came back more radiant than ever. The light of a heavenly bliss lay upon him, if one might say so. Bend-ing down, he whispered softly into my ear as though he were afraid of waking somebody:

"He's asleep, my professor. God grant he has a good sleep, so that he comes down to our place with a fresh head. Now, where did I leave off—at Kashevarovka?

"Well then, I come to Kashevarovka and go straight to the house, ring the bell at the door, once, twice, three times. At last a mug is stuck out, a scraped, well-fed, red mug, that licks its chops like a cat and says in Russian, 'What d'yer want?' And I answer in Jewish, 'I want what I want. If I didn't "want" I wouldn't drag myself here all the way from Kodno.' He listens, chews, licks himself and shakes his head. 'Our people are not receiving anyone. They've got a professor here. . . .' 'All the better,' says I. 'It's the professor I've come for.' And he says, 'What business have you with the professor?' Go and tell him! So then I hand him the letter. 'It's all very well,' I says, 'for you to stand there prattling on the other side of the door while I have to stand out here in the rain. Be kind enough,' I says, 'to give this document to your master at once—into his own hands.' And so I am left out in the street, waiting to be called. I wait half an hour, I wait an hour, two hours. It's raining cats and dogs. No one calls me. I begin to feel sore about it. Not so much on my own account, as on account of our rabbi. After all, the letter is not from some snotty-nose of a boy, but from a rabbi (the Kodno rabbi is known far and wide!). I pull the bell again and again. Out pops the same mug, fuming, and shouts: 'The cheek! What d'yer mean, ringing like that!' 'It's a cheek to keep a man standing in the rain for two hours,' I says. And I step towards the door, wanting to go in. Some hopes. He slams the door right in my face, and that's that. Something's got to be done, though. I wasn't feeling any too cheerful. I didn't like the idea of going back empty-handed at all. Secondly, I felt ashamed for my own sake. After all, I'm a householder of a sort in Kodno, not just anybody. Besides, my heart bled for my poor child.

"But an Almighty God sits on high. What should I see but a four-in hand come driving straight up to the entrance. I ask the coachman, 'What carriage is this, whose horses?' I am told that the carriage is Borodenko's and the horses are Borodenko's. For the professor. To take him to the station. If that's the case, I think, then that's good! That's fine! Before I can look round the door opens and he comes out—the professor himself, a teeny-weeny old man with the face of—what shall I tell you—an angel, a heavenly angel. Itzik Borodenko himself, without a hat on, sees him out, and right behind comes the fellow with the undressed face carrying the professor's bag. You should have seen that rich man, a millionaire almost! May God forgive me for such speeches! He had on him a plain cheap jacket like those we wear in Kodno, kept his hands in his pockets, and his eyes looked nine ways. I was standing and thinking, 'O Heavenly Father! And this creature has millions!' But go and argue with the Lord! When that millionaire caught sight of me he began drilling me with his squint eyes. Then he asks, 'What do you want?' 'Well, it's so-an-so and so-and-so,' I says, 'I brought you a letter from the rabbi.' And he says, 'From what rabbi?' 'The Kodno rabbi,'' I says. 'I'm a Kodno man myself. I've come specially to ask the professor if he wouldn't mind taking the trouble to drop in on us at Kodno on his way back, only for a quarter of an hour, from one train to another, to see my son. My child, God save us, is at death's door.' I told him that straight. I wasn't exaggerating that much, not a grain! What did I figure on? I thought, 'misfortune has befallen the man—his daughter has poisoned herself. Maybe his heart will be softened, and he will take pity on a poor father....' Nothing of the sort! He didn't

say half a word in reply. He squinted at the **great lout**
with the red mug, as much as to say, 'I wish you'd get
rid of this Jew for me.' Meanwhile, that professor of
mine had got into the carriage with his bag. Another
minute and it would be good-bye professor! What's to
be done? Seeing that the whole game was going to the
devil, I suddenly decide—come what may! Something's
got to be done to save the child! So taking my courage
in both hands, I go—flop!—right under the horses'
hooves. To say that I enjoyed lying under the horses'
hooves, I shouldn't say. I don't remember how long I lay
there or whether I lay there at all. Maybe I didn't. All I
know is that it didn't last longer than the moment
it takes me to tell you, because the next moment
the old professor gentleman was standing over me
'What's the matter?' he says. Then adds, 'My dear
man,' giving me to understand, that is, that I should
tell him all about it, get it off my chest. The rich
squinter stands a little to one side eyeing me over
while I am speaking. I don't mind telling you that
I'm no expert at speaking Russian. But this time God
came to my help, and I gave tongue. I told him everything, got the whole thing off my chest. 'It's so-and-so
and so-and-so, sir professor,' I says. 'Maybe you are the
heaven-sent means of saving my child, the last one of
six left to me for many long years. And if, I says, it will
have to cost money, then, please—I have a whole quarter, twenty-five rubles, that is. Not mine, God forbid!
How come I to have such money? It's my wife's. She
was intending to go up to town to buy goods. But who
cares about the quarter, or about my wife's whole shop,
so long as the child can be saved!' I unbutton my capote
while I'm saying this to get out the twenty-five rubles.
But the old gentleman puts his hand on my shoulder—
'Never mind about that!' and tells me to get in with him
in the carriage. May I never live to see my son well if I

am not telling you the truth! Now, I ask you, is Itzik Borodenko worth my professor's little finger? Why, that Borodenko was nearly the ruin of me! It's good that everything turned out well. But what, God forbid, if it hadn't? What then? Eh?"

There was a stir in the carriage, and my companion rushed up to the conductor.

"Kodno?"

"Kodno."

"Good-bye! A happy journey! Please don't tell anyone whom I'm travelling with. I don't want our people in Kodno to know that I'm bringing a professor down. They'll flock down in crowds."

With that confidential request, my companion shook my hand and disappeared.

Several minutes later, when the train had moved on again, I looked out of the window. A rickety old tarantass, drawn by a pair of scrawny sorry-looking greys, drove away from the station. In the tarantass sat a little old gentleman in spectacles, with youthfully ruddy cheeks and a grey little beard. Facing him sat my recent companion, or rather he dangled as if at the end of a string, bouncing up and down over the pot-holes, and peering into the old gentleman's eyes, the while his face beamed and his own eyes bade fair to pop out of his head with joy.

It's a pity I am not a photographer and don't carry a camera about with me. My companion would have made a fine picture at that moment. Let people see what a lucky man looks like—the luckiest man in Kodno.

1909

M E T H U S E L A H

A JEWISH HORSE

THEY CALLED him Methuselah in Kasrilovka because he was stricken in years and had not a single tooth in his head, not counting two or three stumps with which he chewed when he had anything to chew. Tall, scraggy, raw-boned, wall-eyed (one eye was bleached, the other bloodshot), knock-kneed, broken-winded, with sunken flanks, a sagging underlip that gave him an I-am-soon-going-to-cry sort of look, and a skimpy tail—there you have his portrait. And he dwelt in his old age in Kasrilovka, where he did service as a horse with the Kasrilovka water-carrier.

Methuselah was by nature a hardworking, docile animal, worn out, poor devil, by a life of drudgery. After plodding all day through the thick mud of Kasrilovka's streets and providing the little town with its day's supply of water, Methuselah was glad when he was at last unharnessed and tossed an armful of hay followed by a tub of slops for a titbit, which the missus Kasrilichka placed before him with the air of one serving up a dish

158

of fish or a bowl of *vareniki* to the most honoured guest. Methuselah always looked forward to those slops, because they had soaked bits of bread in them, *kasha* leavings and other tasty morsels for which one did not need any teeth. Kasrilichka always thought of Methuselah when she was in the kitchen and threw into the tub everything that came to her hand, so that the poor horse should have something to eat when he came home. And after fortifying himself, Methuselah would turn his face towards his barrel, and his—excuse me—back towards the missus. This was supposed to mean, "Thanks for the wining and the dining." His underlip sagging lower than ever and his one good eye shut, he would become sunk in equine thought.

2

You must not think, however, that Methuselah had always been like this picture we have drawn of him here. Years ago, when he was still a foal trotting after his mother alongside the cart, he had given promise of becoming a brave horse. Connoisseurs had said that he had the makings of a splendid horse. "You wait," they predicted, "he'll run in harness with the finest carriage-horses going!"

When the foal grew up and became a horse, he was unceremoniously bridled and taken out to the fair, where he was put with other horses. About fifty times he was put through his paces, and every minute had his teeth examined and his feet lifted to show his hooves. The end of it was that he passed into strange hands.

That is when his troubles began. He wandered endlessly from place to place, from one master to another, dragged carts with thousand-pound loads, floundered up to his belly in the mud, and had a taste of the lash and the stick laid over his sides, his head and his legs.

3

For a long time he ran as wheeler in a post team with bells that jingled over his ear without a stop—ding-dong! ding-dong!—and rushed backwards and forwards like mad along one and the same high-road. Then he passed into the hands of an ordinary peasant, where he did all the heaviest work, such as ploughing and sowing, hauling huge carts with grain, barrels of water, carts loaded with horse and cow dung, and performed lots of other hard jobs, which he was quite unaccustomed to. From the peasant he passed to a gypsy. The gypsy treated him very shabbily, and did such mean things to him to make him run faster that he would never forget it as long as he lived. From the gypsy he passed into a large drove, and after a while found himself in Mazepovka with the owner of a heavy iron-bound van, over which hung a queer-looking tattered cover. Here, with this drayman, the whips and sticks played over him without a stop, as if a horse's skin were raw-hide leather instead of flesh and blood, and a horse's flanks were made of iron instead of bone. O-ho-ho! How many times did Methuselah stumble along, barely dragging his feet, his haunches racked as if by pincers, in his stomach a heavy weight as if a stone lay there, while his master, that merciless drayman, kept shouting "gee-up!" and "gee-up!", lashing him with the whip and whacking him with the handle. What for, I ask you?!

Luckily that drayman had a custom under which one day in the week you could stand still—just stand there and chew and do nothing. The thing had often puzzled Methuselah. His horse brain simply couldn't grasp the meaning of it. Why was it that nobody bothered you on that day? And why couldn't such a custom be kept for all the other days? Pondering thus, he would shut one eye and glance with the other at his two mates, who stood there hitched to the same van.

4

The drayman and his van were followed by a threshing-machine. Here he came to know gruelling toil. Day in day out, dazed by the clatter of the machine, he trudged round in a circle, swallowing dust and chaff, which got packed into his nostrils, his ears and his eyes. "What's the sense in going round and round like this?" he often asked himself, trying to stop if only for a minute. "Who thought up this clever idea of going round and round on one spot?" But he was given no time for reflection; behind him stood a man with a whip who kept on shouting, "Now then, gee-up there!" "What a fool you are!" Methuselah thought, eyeing the man with the whip. "I'd like to see how you'd go round and round here if I were to hitch you to a wheel and whip you up from behind."

Naturally, what with circling round like that in the everlasting dust, the poor devil soon became an invalid. One eye went blind, the other inflamed, and he got wobbly around the legs. With such obvious faults as these he was fit only for the bone yard. So Methuselah was taken out to the fair again in the hope that somebody would buy him. He was groomed up, his mane was combed, his skimpy tail tied up, and his hooves were greased to make them look fresh. But it was no use—people were not to be taken in. No matter how he was drilled to hold his head high and look a gay spark, he could not be made to do it. He stood with a drooping head, bent knees, and sagging underlip, and even dropped a tear while he was at it. No one cared to buy him any more. One or two men came up, but they did not even examine his teeth; at the sight of his woebegone figure they spat and passed on with a scornful gesture. There was only one man who wanted to buy—not the horse, but its hide. But he couldn't come to terms with the seller. The trader of hides figured that it wasn't worth his while. To take the horse down to the knacker's to be killed and skinned would cost him more than the hide was worth.

But Methuselah, apparently, was destined to have a peaceful old age. The Kasrilovka water-carrier came along and took him home with him to Kasrilovka.

5

Up till then Kasriel—a broad-shouldered hairy-faced man with a squashed nose—had been his own carrier and his own nag, that is, he had simply hitched himself to the barrel cart and delivered the water around the town. And although he had a very hard time of it, Kasriel never envied anybody. Only when he saw a man with a horse did he stop and stand there for a long time gazing after him. One thing he dreamt of all his life—that with God's help he would be able to provide himself with a horse some day. But save as he might, he could never scrape together enough money to buy one. Yet never a fair was held that did not find him jostling there around the horses, feasting his eyes on them. No one charged you anything for looking. And then he had come across that nag, standing dismally in the middle of the market-place without a bridle, without a halter. Kasriel stopped. His heart told him that here at last was a horse which he could afford to buy.

And so it proved to be. He did not have to haggle long. Taking the horse by the bridle, the happy Kasriel all but flew home with it. He knocked, and Kasrilichka came out. She looked frightened.

"What is this? God be with you!"

"I bought it, by my life, I bought it!"

Kasriel and Kasrilichka could not decide where to stable their horse. If they had not been ashamed of their neighbours they would have taken it into the house. In less time than it takes to tell they had procured hay and straw from somewhere, and there they stood in front of the horse—husband and wife, unable to fill their eyes enough with the sight of it.

The neighbours, too, came to have a look at the wonder-horse, which Kasriel had brought home from the market. They poked fun at it and cracked all kinds of jokes, as usual.

"That isn't a horse, it's a mule or something!" one man declared.

"Who said it's a mule? It's a cat!" added another.

A third inserted: "It's just a shadow, you'd better screen it in case the wind, God forbid, blows it away!"

"How old can the thing be?" someone was curious to know.

"Probably older than Kasriel and Kasrilichka put together."

"It's as old as Methuselah!"

And the name of Methuselah had stuck to it ever since.

6

But then Methuselah lived with Kasriel as he had never lived during his best years. For one thing, what kind of work was this? Enough to make a cat laugh! Dragging a barrel of water about and stopping at every house—call that work? And the master! Why, the man was a jewel! He did not even shout loud, did not as much as touch him—held the whip just like that, for show. And the food! True, he did not get oats, but what's the use of oats when you have nothing to chew them with! He much preferred the slops with the soaked bread which Kasrilichka gave him every day. Not so much the slops really as the manner of service. You should see Kasrilichka when she stood there with her arms folded on her bosom, gazing fondly at Methuselah putting away the slops—*tfui, tfui,* may the Evil Eye spare him! And when night came, they made him a litter of straw out in the yard, and then Kasriel or Kasrilichka would come out every few minutes to make sure that no one, God forbid, had stolen him. At peep of dawn, when God Himself is still asleep, the water-carrier is already to be found fussing round his horse. He slowly harnesses him, climbs up on the box and drives down to the river for water, humming to himself a strange tune, "Blessed is he who walketh not...." which is his way of saying how good it is for a man who doesn't have to go on foot. Yet when he goes back with a full barrel Kasriel walks; he doesn't sing to himself then, but plods along through the mud together with Methuselah, just waving his whip and saying, "Come on, Methuselah! Get along, lad!"

Methuselah wades doggedly through the mud, tossing his head, glancing at his master with his one good eye, and thinking to himself, "Ever since I've been a beast I've never had to work for such a queer fellow." And, struck by a sudden thought, the nag begins to limp, then, just for the fun of the thing, stops dead right in the mud. "Let's see what happens!" Seeing the horse suddenly stop, Kasriel starts pottering around the cart, examining the axles, the wheels, the harness, while Methuselah turns his head round towards his master with grinning lips, as if to say, "Well, of all the silly asses this fellow is the silliest!"

7

But there is no lasting joy upon earth. Methuselah could have said that he was happily living out his life with the water-carrier and his wife were it not for the

Kasrilovka children. The neighbours' and all other kinds
of children were a terrible nuisance, a thorn in his side,
the shame of his old age.

From the very first minute that he was brought into the
yard the children conceived for him ... not dislike, God
forbid, but on the contrary—a great affection, an affection
that proved to be fatal to Methuselah. Better had they
loved him less and pitied him more.

The first thing those barefoot pupils of the *Talmud
Torah*, Kasriel's children, did when nobody was about was
to test whether Methuselah could feel like a human being.
They tried hitting him on the back with a stick—nothing; they tickled his leg—nothing; they flicked his ear—
hardly anything; and only when they drew a straw across
his wall-eye did they satisfy themselves that Methuselah
could feel like a human being, because he blinked his
eyes and tossed his head as much as to say, "Anything
but that please! I don't like it." And that being the case,
the children pulled a twig out of the besom and stuck it
right up the horse's nostril. At this Methuselah gave a
start, a jump and a snort.

Out came running Kasriel.

"Murderers! What are you doing to the horse! Off to
school with you, you good-for-nothings!"

And away they scampered to the *Talmud Torah* as
fast as they could lay a leg to the ground.

8

There was a boy at the *Talmud Torah* by the name of
Ruvele, as mischievous and saucy a young imp as ever
was born to plague people. His own mother used to say
of him, "Such as he should be densely sown and thinly
grown!" His favourite pastime was being a nuisance. He
had explored all the lofts and all the cellars in the neighbourhood. Chasing fowls, geese, and ducks, beating dogs,

scaring goats and maltreating cats—not to mention pigs!—was a passion with him. Neither maternal cuffs, nor his teacher's birch, nor even strangers' clumps on the side of the head had any effect. You could scold him as much as you like—it was like peas bouncing off a wall. Only this minute he had got a good hiding and had been weeping bitter tears, but the moment you turn your back—aha!—Ruvele is already showing his tongue, bunching his lips up into a cherry, blowing out his cheeks fit to burst. And his cheeks, I may tell you, were like two rosy little puddings. He was always gay and healthy. What was it to him that his mother, a poor careworn widow, worked her fingers to the bone to be able to pay the ruble for his studies at the *Talmud Torah*!

When Ruvele got to know from Kasriel's children that their father had come home from the market with a horse called Methuselah, he jumped up on the bench, drew first one hand then the other under his nose, and let out a wild yell, "Boys, we've got a bow!"

It should be mentioned that Ruvele had a passion for music ever since he was a little one. He loved musicians and was just crazy about the fiddle.

He had rather a pleasant little voice, too, and knew no end of songs. His one ambition was to grow up and buy himself a fiddle, on which he would play day and night. Meanwhile he had made himself a little fiddle out of wood with cotton threads for strings, and, naturally, had got what was coming to him from his mother.

"A musician you're going to be? May I never live to see it!"

In the evening, after Chaim-Chone the teacher had let his pupils go, they all trooped down in a crowd to see Kasriel's horse. Ruvele promptly declared:

"Methuselah is a splendid horse. His tail will be good for any amount of strings. We'll try it right away."

And Ruvele stole up to Methuselah from the rear and began to pull hairs out of his tail. So long as he pulled them out one by one, Methuselah didn't mind. "One hair?" he seemed to be saying. "Pooh, who cares! One hair more, one less—what does it matter!" But when Ruvele got into his stride and began pulling them out in bunches, Methuselah got angry. "Oh, so that's it, is it? Seat a pig at the table and he'll put his feet on it!" And without thinking twice, Methuselah fetched Ruvele a kick right in the teeth and cut his lip open.

"Serves you right! O woe is me! I'm very glad! That I had ever been born! You'll know better next time! O my curse, my plague!" wailed Ruvele's mother Yenta as she applied a cold compress to her son's gashed lip. She wept, and wrung her hands, and beat her breast, and kept running to Chiene the quack doctress.

9

Ruvele, thank God, was one of those boys who rally from their injuries like a dog. Before you could turn round his lip had healed as if nothing had ever happened. And he was already up to new tricks. The latest idea was for all the pupils to take a ride on Methuselah's back—the whole caboodle. But how was this to be done without anyone knowing? Ruvele decided that it would have to be done on Saturday, when Kasrilovka took its after-dinner nap. You could then carry the whole of Kasrilovka out of the house without waking anybody.

One of the pupils raised a religious objection: "How can a Jew ride on *Shabbas*?" But Ruvele dismissed it with: "Ass, do you call that riding? It's only a game!"

Came Saturday. Everyone had his dinner and laid down for a nap. Kasriel and Kasrilichka lay down too. Thereupon the children began gathering on the quiet in his yard. Ruvele proceeded at once to smarten up Meth-

uselah. First of all he plaited his mane and decorated it
with straws, then he put a white paper cap on his head,
which he fastened down with strings, and finally tied an
old besom to his tail to make it look longer and smarter.
Then the boys, falling over each other in their eagerness,
began clambering up onto the horse's back. Those who
managed to get on, got on, the others had to wait their
turn. Meanwhile they trooped along behind, prodding
Methuselah on to a livelier pace and chanting in chorus:
"For so shall the horse be requitted according to his
deserts!"

Methuselah, however, had no desire to go faster, and
he poked along at an easy pace. For one thing—what
was the hurry? Secondly, that day was a day of rest. But
Ruvele kept egging the horse on without a stop, whoaing,
and tchicking, and honking, and yelling lustily to the
rest of the gang, "What the devil are you thinking of!
Why don't you make a noise?"

But Methuselah just jogged along at a foot pace, thinking to himself, "The children are just having their
fun—no harm in that!"

But when the boys got troublesome and started driving, yelling and waving their arms, he mended his gait;
and when he did that the besom started slapping his legs.
At that he broke into a run. The besom started slapping
harder. Methuselah went into a gallop. The children were
delighted. As for Ruvele, he jumped up and down for joy,
yelling all the time, "Hop-hop-hop!" They hopped along
till they started dropping off the horse's back like so many
dumplings. And Methuselah, stimulated by a sense of
new-found freedom, tore along like mad, making a dash
for the open country beyond the windmill.

Here the shepherd boys, seeing a queerly decked horse
in a paper cap gave chase with loud whoops, threw
sticks at it and set the dogs on it. The dogs needed no
second invitation. They went after Methuselah in full cry,

snapping and tearing; some got their teeth into his haunches from behind, others dashed forward and flung themselves at his throat. Methuselah began to make queer strangled noises. The dogs worried him until he was dead.

10

The next day the boys were given their deserts. Bumps and bruised noses do not count. On top of this they got it hot both from their parents and from their teacher, Chaim-Chone. Ruvele, of course, caught it worse than anybody else, because all the boys cried when they got a caning, as boys usually do, whereas this one, on the contrary, laughed. That made him get it still harder. But the harder he was flogged the more did he laugh, and the more he laughed the harder was he flogged. The end of it was that the teacher himself began to laugh, and with him all the pupils. They laughed so much that all the neighbours came running up and passers-by stopped in the street—men and women, boys and girls. "What's up? What's the laughter about? What are they laughing for?" But no one could answer them—everyone was laughing. So then the neighbours and the passers-by started laughing too. At this the pupils and their teacher went off still worse; and, looking at them, the neighbours and passers-by held their sides. In a word, everyone was in stitches, everyone was roaring, howling, weeping with laughter.

Only two people did not laugh—the water-carrier and his wife. When a child, God forbid, dies in the house, I don't know whether his people mourn him half as much as Kasriel and Kasrilichka mourned the loss of their poor horse, old Methuselah.

1902

GLOSSARY

Baal-shem: Literally, Master of the Name; a holy man who was supposed to work wonders by using the name of God.

balagula: A Jewish izvozchik (driver).

baltakse: A collector of taxes in the Jewish community appointed by the rabbi.

Bar Mitzvah: Confirmation ceremony; also a thirteen-year-old Jewish boy who is confirmed.

beigel: A ring-shaped roll of bread.

Bes Hamedresh: A synagogue where pious Jews studied the Talmud.

borshch: A Russian vegetable soup.

cheder: Orthodox Hebrew school.

dayan: A kind of rabbi who renders decisions.

dybbuk: An evil spirit possessing a human being; the soul of a dead person residing in another's body and acting through it.

gabai: The head of a synagogue.

gubernator: A governor in old Russia.

ispravnik: The highest police official of a district in old Russia.

kabtzen: A poor person.

kasha: Groats.

kosher: Food that may be eaten as ritually clean.

maggid: A man who lectures in synagogues.

matzos: Unleavened bread eaten at the Passover.

melamed: Orthodox Hebrew teacher.

meshumad: Apostate, recreant.

metsiah: A bargain.

medresh: An exposition of the Hebrew Scriptures; cited by pious and learned Jews in Talmudic dispute.

mishpocha: The family, kinsmen.

nash: A titbit.

noggid: A rich man, usually leading citizen of a community.

pan: Gentleman, sir; form or address used for Polish landowners.

pristav: A police officer in old Russia.
rebbitzin: The wife of a rabbi.
shabbas: Sabbath (Saturday).
shadchan: Professional match-maker.
shammes: Beadle, sexton.
shlimazl: A "poor stick," one who is dogged by bad luck.
Shma-Koleinu: "Hear our voices!" The opening words of a Day
    of Atonement prayer; also a popular idiom meaning "idiot."
Shma Yisroel: The opening words in the Jewish confession of
    faith: "Hear, O Israel, the Lord is our God, the Lord is One!"
shochet (pl. *shochtim*)*:* Ritual slaughterer of animals for use as
    food in accordance with Jewish laws.
shool: Synagogue.
Simchas Torah: A Jewish holiday celebrating the completion of the
    reading of the Torah.
Succos: Feast of Tabernacles.
tallis: Praying-shawl.
tallis-kot'n: Undergarment with tassels on its four corners worn
    by orthodox Jews.
Talmud Torah: A school for poor Jewish children.
tfillin: Phylacteries.
tsimmes: A sweet side-dish made of carrots and noodles.
vareniki: Curd or fruit dumplings.
yeshiva: Talmudic college.
Yom Kippur: The Day of Atonement, most important Jewish
    religious holiday, observed as a solemn fast day.
yom-tev: Holiday.